The Terrible Tide

By Alisa Craig

THE TERRIBLE TIDE

MURDER GOES MUMMING

THE GRUB-AND-STAKERS MOVE A MOUNTAIN

A PINT OF MURDER

The Terrible Tide

ALISA CRAIG

PUBLISHED FOR THE CRIME CLUB

BY

DOUBLEDAY & COMPANY, INC.

GARDEN CITY, NEW YORK

1983

All the characters in this book are fictitious,
and any resemblance to actual persons,
living or dead,
is purely coincidental.

Library of Congress Cataloging in Publication Data

Macleod, Charlotte.
The Terrible Tide.

I. Title.
PS3563.A31865T4   1983   813'.54
ISBN 0-385-18700-9
Library of Congress Catalog Card Number 82-45867

First Edition

For the Radles

The Terrible Tide

Chapter 1

"Watch it, Fan," cried Holly. "You're popping your seams."

"I don't give a damn. Heave on this crowbar, can't you?"

Fan Howe was panting. Sweat beaded her blotchy red forehead. More stitches burst in the brown pants suit she'd bought three years ago at a Westchester shopping mall. Now it was baggy, stained, fuzzed with enough catches to make her look like a worn-out Teddy bear.

"I'm heaving as hard as I can, Fan. You know I shouldn't be doing this. They told me at the hospital to take it easy."

"You can't baby yourself forever," Fan snapped back. "Come on, put some beef in it."

"Three weeks out after four weeks in isn't exactly babying myself. Anyway, vandalism's not my thing."

"Holly, for God's sake! These old farmhouses are abandoned, falling apart. Why let good lumber lie around and rot? Roger needs it."

That was the clincher. What Roger Howe needed, Roger got, even if his wife and sister had to fight, steal, and wade through acres of poison ivy to find it for him. When Roger had decided to leave the bank and devote himself to his real love, which was certainly not Fan but the reproducing of fine antique furniture, Fan had left her comfortable home in a fashionable New York suburb and immigrated to Canada without a whimper.

Moving to New Brunswick had made sense, back in Westchester. The province had gorgeous scenery and status as a center for arts and crafts. Moreover, Roger and Holly had inherited a house there from some relatives they'd never seen. At that time, they hadn't seen the property, either.

Holly herself had never set eyes on the place Fan had grandly rechristened Howe Hill until she'd needed a quiet place to recuperate and decided she might as well claim her half-share of its amenities. She'd soon found out there weren't any, except for a handsome view of the Bay of Fundy and its incredible tides. The house was almost as derelict as the one she and Fan were dismantling now. Holly was still stunned at Fan's calm acceptance of its discomforts and inconveniences for the sake of Roger and his art.

She was also astonished by her brother's emergence as a master craftsman. That he was still the self-centered cold fish she'd known and mildly disliked since she could remember came as no surprise at all.

Nobody could actively hate Roger Howe. He never did anything rotten, at least not on purpose. His manners were courteous even when they didn't have company. When he remembered to say anything at all, he made the right sorts of noises. On the surface, Roger was a model husband and a fair enough brother, but if Holly'd realized what he was really like to live with, she'd have stayed far, far away from Howe Hill.

How could she have known? Born fifteen years apart to career-oriented parents, she and he had never been given much chance to get acquainted. When she was little, Holly had met her big brother now and then on stopovers between school and summer camp. She had vague memories of a tall youth, handsomer than she'd ever be, who'd stayed in his room assembling model airplanes and never said anything to her except, "Don't touch my tools." Why couldn't he be here to say it now?

Goaded to desperation, Holly threw all her weight on the hateful crowbar. Rusty nails gave with a screech. Fan whooped.

"Look at that! Roger will swoon for joy."

Holly doubted that. She'd never seen her brother joyful, not even at his wedding, where she'd been forced to wear a silly pink ruffled gown and a Little-Bo-Peep bonnet. She'd thrown up in the bonnet at the reception to show them they couldn't make a fool of her and get away with it.

After that, Roger and Fan had been rather standoffish with Holly until they'd met again at the funeral. Their parents had been killed in a car smash. Holly had cried because she'd always hoped some day her mother and father would stick around long enough so she could get to know them, and now she never would. Roger had shown only a decent gravity until he'd found out his only legacy was a few thousand dollars and half-interest in the Canadian farmhouse. Then he'd blown his stack.

"Come on," Fan was urging. "Let's get the rest of it."

Sighing, Holly picked up the wrecking bar and tried to dig it in behind what must once have been a charming overmantel.

"Not that way! You'll splinter the wood." Fan grabbed the tool and worked it skillfully under the wide board.

"Good work, Fan. You're quite a demolition expert."

"I ought to be. I've done enough of it by now."

Fan wasn't complaining, merely stating a fact. Maybe she was happier in Jugtown than she'd been back in Westchester. There she'd played the model housewife, angling for Roger's praise and getting only his calm acceptance. Here she could wallow in valiant self-sacrifice as she battled tooth and claw to make her husband's dream come true.

Roger ought to be pleased by today's haul, assuming he had no qualms about receiving stolen property. Anyway, Fan didn't seem to need so many pats on the head as she used to. She'd made up her mind she was married to a genius. Everybody knew what wives of great men had to go through before they got to write their memoirs. Fan was already compiling her scrapbook.

Holly might come in for a paragraph or two. "My sister-in-law, tragically disfigured by the accident that ended her career as a professional model—"

Nuts to that. Holly wasn't going to be disfigured. At least not permanently. Anyway, not much. She'd get back into modeling.

Sure she would. The scars on her face and body had to heal before plastic surgery could begin. Then there'd be more healing, and by then she'd have lost her contacts. The flesh machine would have ground out too many fresher, smoother, prettier, younger girls. She was a has-been at twenty-one, and she might as well admit it.

Right now, Holly didn't care as much as she'd thought she would. Modeling was just something she'd drifted into because her half of the inheritance hadn't been enough to send her to college. She'd done some fashion shows, then wound up in front of a camera because she was tall and skinny and had good cheekbones. Having no illusions about her beauty or talent, she'd been untemperamental to work with. Photographers liked her vivid blue eyes, her habit of turning up on schedule with her face already fixed and her light brown hair already combed. They'd begun steering better assignments her way. She'd been on the way up, until she'd been so suddenly and agonizingly brought down. Well, back to the wrecking bar.

They were in luck. The nail holes had rotted out and the panel came off without a struggle. Holly was all for quitting then and there, but Fan insisted they stay and rescue as many as they could of the old hand-forged nails.

That was a tedious, touchy job. If pulled too fast or bent too far, the nails would snap off. Holly broke two, then left the rest to Fan and went to stare out the window. This was beautiful country, if only she didn't have to view it while listening to her sister-in-law's groaning and muttering. She tried to concentrate on the birds flitting among the tangled briars she and Fan would soon have to fight their way through to where they'd hidden the truck. All at once, something else caught her attention.

"What do you know? We're going to have company."

"Who? Where? Quick, get back from that window."

"What for? I thought you said we weren't doing anything wrong."

"Don't be funny." Fan elbowed Holly out of the way and peeked anxiously through the spider-webbed pane. "It's okay, they're turning—well, can you beat that?"

"Beat what?" Holly managed to catch a glimpse over Fan's head before the two walkers disappeared. All she learned was that the woman had glossy black hair and the man was wearing a tweed cap and a blue plaid shirt. "What's so exciting? Do you know them?"

"I know her." Fan's face was one vast, malicious grin. "So this is why she takes long walks in the country. For exercise, she says. I'll bet that guy gives her plenty."

"Goody gumdrops, a scandal. Who is she?"

"Claudine Parlett, the village virgin, or so we've been led to believe. She runs an antique shop and everything else she can poke her nose into. Come on, we'd better leave in case they take a notion to come back. Not that way, stupid! Out the side door."

Holly was only too happy to obey. They wrestled their booty through brush and briar to the Howes' old truck and stowed it under a dirty tarpaulin in case a shower happened to come up and soak the wood. At that moment there was only one tiny cloud in the whole, vast, late-summer sky. As Fan said, though, you couldn't be too careful.

Chapter 2

Fan entertained herself all the way home wondering whose husband Claudine Parlett was sneaking out to meet. Since all the husbands in Jugtown dressed pretty much alike in tweed caps and plaid shirts, she had a wide-open field for speculation.

Holly, not knowing any of the men and not giving a hoot anyway, sat gritting her teeth against the lurches and yearning for the hot bath she wouldn't be able to take. The Howes still hadn't been able to afford indoor plumbing.

When they'd made their decision to sell out of the Establishment and move to the Good Life, Fan and Roger had been dismayed to find they really hadn't much to sell. They'd played the status-symbol game like their neighbors even though Roger's salary at the bank had been barely adequate to keep them afloat. Their equity in the Westchester house had been next to nil. Furnishings they couldn't afford to ship had been sacrificed for whatever they'd bring. They'd practically been down to living on roots and berries before Roger landed his first and only customer.

They were still struggling to make ends meet. Holly's contribution to the weekly housekeeping money was already making a difference in the standard of living at Howe Hill. It was as well Fan and Roger didn't know how little was left of that fabulous model's income she'd supposedly been making. Holly had a pretty clear idea of how welcome she'd be once her cash ran out. If she was forced to leave before she healed, though, where could she go?

At least the hideous ride was over. Fan swung the rattling truck into the weedy, unkempt dooryard. Holly tried to heave herself out of the van. The deep slash on her left thigh, kept unhealed and inflamed by overexertion, gave such a wicked twinge that she fell back on the seat with a yelp.

"Hold on, let me give you a hand."

That was Roger's lone assistant, Bert Walker, the only one around here who ever appeared to remember that Holly was a human being with genuine medical problems. In fact, for an old gaffer who looked, smelled, and often talked like a hobo, Bert could show surprising gallantry. Holly sometimes wondered what his history had been. In any event, as long as she managed to keep upwind of him, Holly enjoyed Bert's company more than anyone else's she'd met so far in Jugtown.

Bert was her authority on local history. According to him, the first settlers were Loyalists who fled Boston around 1776. Among them were potters who sailed up the Bay of Fundy looking for a clay pit at which to establish themselves as makers of fine chinaware. They'd found some clay; but soon learned nobody in this wilderness cared about fine china, only heavy crocks to salt down their food in, and sturdy jugs to hold their drink.

Since the growing season was shorter than the drinking season, jugs sold better than crocks. Within a few years, the potters were concentrating on this one profitable item, and their settlement had become known as Jugtown.

The clay pit had been worked out long ago, but Jugtown hung on. Nowadays some of the locals were trying to capitalize on its quaint name, hoping to attract more tourists. So far, they hadn't. The antique dealers, the knitters and weavers and rug hookers, the whittlers who carved little sea gulls and perched them on bits of driftwood still had to rely on shops in more popular resort areas as outlets. Right now, Roger Howe seemed to be the only craftsman around who wasn't worrying about where he could sell his products.

Fan took credit for the recent upturn in the Howes' fortunes.

It was she who'd pawned her engagement ring to pay for advertisements in a couple of antique collectors' magazines, and it was through one of those ads that they'd got in touch with Mrs. Brown.

Mrs. Brown, according to what Holly had been able to gather from Fan, was an interior decorator who specialized in doing period rooms for the rich and the even richer. Since fine antiques were becoming so scarce, Mrs. Brown sometimes had to resort to reproductions.

Naturally, such clients as hers would never be satisfied with ordinary commercial copies. Even the wealthiest and fussiest, however, couldn't cock a nostril at an expertly handcrafted replica of an authentic museum piece, made with eighteenth-century tools and techniques, using the same well-seasoned woods and even the same smelly glues that might have been found in the workshops of Samuel McIntire or Duncan Phyfe.

Roger had become one of Mrs. Brown's trade secrets. She'd promised to give him all the work he could handle, provided he stopped running ads so that her competitors wouldn't know where she was getting her fabulous reproductions. So far, she'd kept her word. For over a year now, Roger had been supplied with orders, including sketches, detailed explanations, and exact descriptions of what Mrs. Brown wanted, at such a rate that he was always behind schedule.

Because of his time-consuming methods and his fanatical insistence on absolute fidelity to every detail, Roger had lagged to a point where he'd been forced to get help with some of the less-exacting work. He was paying Bert Walker on a day-to-day basis out of the American cash with which Mrs. Brown always settled her sizable bills. At first Holly thought this was just sloppy business practice. Now that she knew where Roger got his lumber, she thought perhaps there was more to it than sloppiness.

Fan must be bursting to show Roger the magnificent slabs of solid walnut they'd ripped off, but she wouldn't remove the tarpaulin while Bert was still around. He'd be too apt to recognize whose parlor the paneling had come from. Holly would have liked to keep the handyman chatting awhile, just to get back at Fan for making her help, but she was in no shape for conversation. Moving stiffly because her leg was hurting so much, she started toward the house.

"I'm going to lie down for a while."

"Oh?" Roger was cool and courteous as always. "I thought you might enjoy helping Fan fix dinner."

"I can manage by myself," snapped his wife. "I always do, don't I?"

"Stop it!"

The resentment that had been boiling up ever since Holly'd got here finally spilled over. "Listen to me, both of you. When I wrote about coming up here, I explained that I'd been badly injured and needed to rest. You told me to come ahead and take it easy, but from the minute I got here, you've been running me like a pack horse. If I'd known what you had in mind, I'd have gone someplace where I'd at least get paid for doing it instead of slaving my guts out and paying board on top of it, in a house that's as much mine as yours. All right, Fan. Now that you've tried to land me back in the hospital and set me up for a charge of breaking and entering, what's next on the agenda? Do I peel the potatoes or rob the town bank?"

Roger and Fan were both making shushing gestures, rolling their eyes at Bert, who was enjoying the scene hugely. Roger started a speech about giving his sister a richer experience of life in Jugtown. Fan fussed around being solicitous and placatory. Bert said the only thing that made sense.

"They need a hired girl out at Cliff House."

All three quit squabbling and said, "What?" in unison.

"Mrs. Parlett's still hangin' on out there by the toenails. Claudine was on to me about 'er Saturday when I went to pick up the groceries for Annie, askin' if I knew anybody willin' to help out."

"Doing what?"

The handyman had begun fiddling with his braces buckles,

embarrassed for some reason. "Help Annie shove a little gruel into 'er three times a day an' change 'er nightgown, I s'pose. She can't do a hand's turn for herself, poor soul."

"Why? Does she have some awful disease?"

"Yep. I got it, too. Old age."

Bert didn't haul off the joke with his usual gusto. What was he so fidgety about all of a sudden?

"Who's Annie?" Holly prodded. "Her daughter?"

"Nope. I guess likely you'd call 'er the housekeeper. Annie's been at Cliff House long as I can remember."

"Then Annie must be an old woman, too. Is that why Claudine wants more help out there?"

"That's it." Bert welcomed the explanation like a long-lost brother. "Claudine don't think them two ought to be out there by their lonesomes, not now."

"How much does the job pay?"

"Claudine didn't say. Not much, most likely. You'd get your board an' keep."

"I'll take it." Anything was better than helping Fan tear Jugtown apart. "What do I do, just barge in and start changing nightgowns?"

Bert seemed to be experiencing a strange mixture of relief and alarm. "You better talk to Claudine first. Her an' Ellis are the next o' kin, not that blood's any thicker'n water in that fam'ly. Anyway, Mrs. Parlett's only their great-aunt by marriage, though it wouldn't cut much ice either way, I don't s'pose. Yep, you talk to Claudine. I got to get home to my supper. You want me in the mornin', Roger?"

"As early as possible, please. I've had another letter from Mrs. Brown about that Sheraton highboy, and I haven't even finished the piecrust tables yet. Fan, I wish you would kindly try to make Mrs. Brown understand I am not a furniture factory."

"Roger, we mustn't antagonize her."

"I have no wish to antagonize her. I merely want her to understand that I am not a machine. The carving on that highboy alone will take a week, perhaps longer."

"Can't Bert help you with it?"

"Bert is not a master woodcarver."

"Jack of all trades an' master o' none, that's me," said the ancient. "I never carved nothin' fancier than a half-moon in the door of a backhouse. You want fancy carvin', you talk to my nephew."

"Then talk to him, Roger!"

Holly heard in Fan's cry the same end-of-the-rope despair that had set off her own outburst. Roger, for a wonder, must have caught it, too. At any rate, he didn't brush off Bert's suggestion with his usual silent disdain of the idea that anybody else could come up to his standards.

"What sort of carving does this nephew do, Bert?"

"Started out makin' signs, an' quarterboards for yachts. Then it got so they was sendin' for him all over Canada. If somebody wants a special job, like the linenfold panelin' for that big estate in Toronto, Sam goes an' does it. Carved statues for a cathedral in Quebec; all sorts o' stuff. He's been commissioned to do some work in Ottawa before the next Royal visit if this dratted gov'ment quits horsin' around an' votes the money."

"There, Roger," said Holly. "If he's good enough for Queen Elizabeth, he ought to be able to satisfy Mrs. Brown."

"Perhaps. He first has to satisfy me. I'm willing to talk to your nephew, Bert. I suppose he's off on some affair of state at the moment?"

Bert either didn't notice Roger's sarcasm or didn't think it worth bothering about. "Nope. Matter of fact, Sam came home last night. Goin' to stick around till his mother gets out o' the hospital. Lorraine's goin' to Saint John for some operation. Don't ask me what, eh. I never pay no attention to women's ailments. Sam might be as well pleased to while away the time helpin' you out 'stead o' settin' around doin' nothin'."

Bert clambered into a pickup truck even more decrepit than

the Howes' and clattered off down the rutted lane. Roger stepped back inside the workshop. Fan and Holly went over to the house.

"Holly, you go and rest," said Fan. "I don't need help. Roger was just being overprotective of me. He still thinks I'm his sweet little girl bride."

She emitted a deprecating whinny, trying to make the fantasy sound halfway plausible. Poor Fan! Holly couldn't help showing some compassion.

"Not many men have wives like you, Fan. I can see how devoted Roger is."

She didn't have to say what Roger was devoted to. Fan was happy enough with the remark as it stood. Deciding she'd done her good deed for the day, Holly limped off to clean up and snatch a little rest.

Chapter 3

The Howes were very polite to each other at dinner. Roger and Fan made mild attempts to persuade Holly she shouldn't take the job at Cliff House. They talked about Holly's own welfare. What they meant was that Roger didn't like the idea of his sister's working as a domestic in Jugtown, and Fan didn't want to lose Holly's weekly board money.

Holly wasn't fooled by Roger's harping on her being company for Fan, either. Without her around, he wouldn't have the relief of being spared some of Fan's incessant bidding for notice. It must have been tough on both husband and wife these past three years, stuck here alone together, each wanting what the other wouldn't give.

For a wonder, Fan didn't say a word about having seen Claudine Parlett in the woods with a man. Could she possibly suspect the man had been Roger? Of course not, how could she? Roger would never do anything so human. Anyway, how could he have got so far from the shop and beaten them back to it? The only transportation at Howe Hill was the truck Fan had been driving.

Still, Roger did have a tweed cap and a plaid shirt, and the man had been tall. Tallish, anyway. Who cared? Holly went to bed as soon as the dishes were done. By morning, Fan and Roger had talked themselves into thinking they could make the Jugtowners believe Holly only wanted the job at Cliff House to keep her from being too bored while she convalesced. Fan was all ready to drive her downtown for the interview with Claudine.

"I suppose you know where to go," Holly remarked as they turned into Queen Street.

"Oh sure, it's right here on the main drag. Claudine turned her folks' house into an antique shop. I guess I told you that yesterday. She and her brother live upstairs."

"Maybe it was the brother we saw her with yesterday."

"Not on your life. Ellis is one of those gangly teenage types, all hands and feet with hair straggling down over his neck."

"Anyway, they keep the place looking nice," Holly said to change the subject. There were boxes of marigolds and trailing vinca below the many-paned bow window. Inside was a charming display of bone china.

"That's Claudine's doing. Ellis spends his time scavenging for junk he can fix up and palm off on the tourists. They do all right, one way and another. I couldn't say how well, of course. Claudine's close-mouthed about her affairs in more ways than one."

Holly didn't want to hear any more about that. She let herself down from the van and entered the showroom, Fan chugging at her heels. They found Claudine selling a luster pitcher to a customer, figuring with a pencil on a paper bag.

"With the exchange, that comes to forty-eight dollars and thirty-two cents in American money."

The prosperous-looking woman who wanted the pitcher fished an ostrich skin wallet out of her suede handbag and started counting out money. "Twenty, forty, five, six, seven, eight. And three dimes. I don't seem to have any—wait a second, I always have pennies at the bottom of my bag. No, I'm afraid I don't. Exactly two cents short."

She laughed gaily, confidently, expecting to be told, "Forget it." Instead, Claudine picked up the pitcher and set it back on the shelf. The customer turned red, scooped the money into her purse, wheeled furiously, and stalked out of the shop. Claudine turned to Fan, her face a polite blank.

"Fan Howe. You're quite a stranger."

Fan, still goggle-eyed at the way Claudine had thrown away

a fifty-dollar sale for two lousy cents, giggled self-consciously. "I know. Somehow, I never find the time to get to meetings."

Claudine gave that remark the silent contempt it deserved. She just stood there. Fan wasted no more breath on small talk.

"This is my sister-in-law, Holly Howe, who's staying with us. Bert Walker says you need somebody to help out at Cliff House, and Holly thought it might be a way to pass the time."

Claudine raised one well-shaped eyebrow. She'd be quite good-looking, Holly thought, if she ever cracked a smile.

"News does get around, doesn't it? Have you any nursing experience, Miss Howe?"

"None whatever." Holly could be brusque, too. "But I've just spent a month in the hospital, as you may have guessed from my scars, and I know the routines. I can't do heavy work yet, but I can cook and keep house after a fashion, and you don't need a nursing degree to empty a bedpan. Your aunt isn't really sick, is she? Bert gave us to understand she's just old and incapable."

"And so's the woman who's supposed to take care of her," Fan put in with her usual tact.

At that, Claudine's poker-face softened. "Annie Blodgett's an angel straight out of heaven. I don't know what I'd ever do without her."

"I'm not trying to steal anybody's job," Holly began.

Claudine wasn't listening. Like the rest of them, she had something to get off her chest.

"Poor Annie. Cliff House is the only home she's known since she was a little girl. She took care of Cousin Edith and Great-aunt Maude and Great-uncle Jonathan and Great-aunt Mathilde, and now she needs somebody to look after her. If Earl Stoodley had his way, she'd be out in the road and my great-aunt in a nursing home, but I won't stand for that and he knows it. I'm as much a trustee as he is, and I'll fight him as long as there's a breath left in me. But something's got to be done. God knows what might happen out there, one lying helpless and the other not much better. It's terrible for me, not being able to go and see for myself how things stand."

But why shouldn't Claudine go if she wanted to? Fan had driven out around Parlett's Point once so that Holly could see Cliff House, which was the best Jugtown could offer as a sightseeing tour. As Holly recalled, the big Victorian gothic house was only a few miles out of town. If Claudine could prowl the hinterlands with her boyfriend, why couldn't she walk that comparatively short distance along a good, paved road?

"Well, I can't let things run on any longer," Claudine was saying. "You may as well give it a try. Keep her clean and fed. That's all anybody can do for her now."

Claudine's voice wavered on those last few words. Holly thought she was actually going to break down, but she didn't.

"I don't know what you expect for wages. Earl wouldn't stand for more than fifty a week plus your room and board, I do know that. It's not much, but it's a case of take it or leave it. He won't spend a penny more than he can help, and he grudges even that little bit."

Holly felt sorry for Claudine, though she wasn't sure why. "I'm not too concerned about the money. As Fan mentioned, I'm mainly looking for something to do till my scars heal. At least there won't be many people out there staring at me." She tried to laugh.

Claudine nodded. "That's true. Nobody will see you but Annie and Bert Walker, unless Earl Stoodley chooses to barge in and throw his weight around. Bert does the chores every night, but he never goes beyond the kitchen. Nobody does. You remember that."

"Not even the doctor?"

"We don't bother the doctor. What's the use? All right then, Holly. I'll phone up and tell Annie you're coming. You go pack your belongings. And I presume you understand once you're there, you stay. Annie needs a person who's going to be around when she's needed, not running back and forth to the village every time she takes the notion."

"I couldn't run if I wanted to," Holly snapped back. "Shall I take my own towels and bedding, or what?"

At that, Claudine managed a bleak smile. "I expect there's linen at Cliff House the moths haven't eaten yet. You're not going to any resort hotel, you know. Cliff House was a beautiful place in its day, but it's pretty rundown now. It's still filled with beautiful things, though, which is why we have to be so particular about no visitors. Even relatives," she added, with a tight-lipped glance at Fan.

Fan shrugged. "Take it easy, Claudine. I know better than to gate-crash. Bert tells me that old housekeeper keeps Cliff House locked up like a fortress."

"She'd better. Don't you ever forget, Holly. Nobody sets foot in that house except the fire brigade, God forbid, if they should ever be needed. You can't keep Earl Stoodley out because he's the other trustee, but don't let him near Mrs. Parlett. He's itching for her to die so he can start his stupid museum and get his fat face in the papers. I wouldn't put it past him to accidentally drop a pillow over her face, or open the windows in the hope she'd catch pneumonia. And if that's defamation of character, I couldn't care less. You can start tomorrow morning."

She glanced at the door. The Howes took the hint. Once outside, Holly burst into half-hysterical giggles.

"What have I got myself into? Is she always like that?"

"Pretty much," said Fan. "Did you notice how she got in a dig at me for not showing up at the Women's Circle? I went a few times when I first came up here, but I soon saw it wasn't going to help Roger any, so now I don't bother."

Holly had other things to think of than the Women's Circle. "What did she mean about that Earl Stoodley and his museum?"

"Mrs. Parlett's willed Cliff House to the town after she goes. Earl Stoodley's got this bee in his bonnet about turning it into one of those historic homes people pay to see. He claims that'll attract more tourists to Jugtown and be good for business. I must say it sounds reasonable to me."

"But would anybody actually come to see the place? Jugtown's awfully off the beaten path."

"Stoodley claims the house is full of genuine antiques. Maybe you can sneak me in for a peek on Annie's day off."

Fan pretended to be joking, but Holly could see sticky times coming. Having seen what Fan could do to unguarded premises, she wasn't about to risk turning her sister-in-law loose at Cliff House. She changed the subject.

"Why's Mrs. Parlett leaving Cliff House to the town instead of to Claudine and her brother?"

"Because they've had a big fight over something or other. Somebody at the Women's Circle told me Claudine vowed never to darken the door again as long as Mrs. Parlett was alive. From what she said just now, I guess she meant it."

"So instead she sits down here and frets herself into a state because she can't go to see Mrs. Parlett. That makes sense!"

"Don't kid yourself. Why should Claudine fret about what happens to Mrs. Parlett? She's not going to get anything out of her."

But she did care. Fan couldn't have noticed how close the antique dealer had come to breaking down. Fan never did notice much that wasn't connected with Roger's needs. Right now she was heading for the grocery store, wondering aloud how she was going to stretch their meager food budget over those seven elegant little dinners Roger expected to be served every week, not to mention breakfasts and lunches. What a life for a woman brought up to affluence!

Fan did appear to be genuinely distressed at the prospect of Holly's moving out to Cliff House. Maybe it was just Holly's board money she was going to miss, but what the heck?

"Look, Fan," Holly said, "I'm not taking all my stuff out there, till I see how things are going to work out. How about if I go on paying you, say twenty-five dollars a week, to keep it for me? That way if the deal falls flat and I have to come back in a hurry, I won't feel I'm imposing on you. Does that sound fair?"

It wasn't fair at all, in fact. Holly had every right to leave her own things in her own half of the house. Fan naturally didn't see it that way. She was just glad and relieved.

"Sure, Holly. It sounds fine. Look, any time you need a ride or anything, let me know."

"There's one thing you can do for me right now." It had occurred to Holly that she might have to pass a lot of boring hours at Cliff House. "Mind dropping me at the public library, if there is one? If I'm going to be stuck out there with two old women, I'll need something to keep me entertained."

"They must have books in the house." Nevertheless, Fan made a detour and pulled up in front of a squarish building with ivy marching in well-disciplined ranks across its red-brick walls.

Holly opened its door on a smell she always enjoyed: dust and paper and printers' ink, with gentle overtones of dry rot. Models spend a lot of time sitting around waiting, so she'd developed a passion for reading. Now that she couldn't squander money on paperbacks, she might as well make use of the public facilities, such as they might be.

In fact, Jugtown had a pretty good library, for its size. Holly had no trouble selecting some good novels and a couple of biographies she'd been wanting to read. Getting the librarian to let her take them out was another matter.

"I'm sorry, but you must have a library card."

"Then could I have one, please?"

"Certainly, if you're a local resident. Just fill out this form and your card will be ready by Wednesday."

"But I don't think I'll be able to come then."

The librarian must be a relative of Claudine Parlett. She didn't exactly snatch the books away, but she didn't look very unbending, either. Holly tried another angle.

"Perhaps I could take them on my brother's card or his

wife's? I'm staying out at Howe Hill with Mr. and Mrs. Roger Howe."

The librarian flipped through her file. "Neither of them is on our list of borrowers."

Holly might have known. Roger had his own reference books on antique furniture, he never looked at anything else, and where would Fan find the time to read? She was about to admit defeat when an unexpected rescuer appeared.

"You may use my card, Miss Howe, if you'll forgive the liberty. I'm Geoffrey Cawne, and I have had the pleasure of meeting your people, though less often than I'd like. You won't mind, will you, Marie?"

"Not if you don't, Professor." The librarian smiled at him as she stamped the books and handed them across the desk.

"Thank you so much," Holly told her sweetly, "and thank you, Professor Cawne. I do appreciate it, and I'll be sure to return them on time."

"I have every confidence in you," he assured her in a voice that was a pleasant blend of academic precision and human warmth. "Now can I offer you a lift to Howe Hill? I'm a neighbor of sorts, you know. My house is that odd-looking gray one on the knoll just before the curve in the road. You may not have noticed because it sits rather far back."

"I certainly have, and I love it. My sister-in-law is picking me up on her way back from getting the groceries. Otherwise, I'd be glad to ride with you."

She would have. Geoffrey Cawne was the kind of professor who made college freshmen—the female ones—swoon on the spot. He was an inch or so taller than she, which would bring him close to six feet. Shell-rimmed glasses added just the right note of strength to what might have been almost too blandly attractive a face. His slacks were handsome Crombie tweed; his cardigan knit of the finest New Brunswick homespun. He must be twice her own age, but Holly couldn't help wondering if there was a Mrs. Cawne in that ultramodern gray house. Not that it would do her much good if there wasn't. A man like

Cawne wasn't apt to be much interested in a mangled assistant housemaid, if that was what she'd so recently become.

Anyway, they stood chatting about nothing in particular until Fan's truck stopped outside with a squeal and a loud honking. After a hurried goodbye, Holly grabbed her books and ran.

Fan leaned over to open the door for her. "Did you get what you wanted?"

"Yes, and I met a friend of yours."

"Didn't know I had one." Fan didn't ask who it was. The truck, always temperamental, had picked this time to stall.

"His name is Cawne," Holly persisted. "He says he's a neighbor."

"Geoffrey Cawne?" Fan quit fiddling with the ignition long enough to stare at her. "You mean he actually came up and spoke to you?"

"He let me use his library card."

"I'll be darned! You may not know it, but you've been honored. Cawne's our local celebrity. He's a famous writer."

"I'm not surprised. He looks the type. What does he write?" Fan shrugged. "I don't know, but he's well-known in his field."

Holly didn't ask what his field was. If Fan had known, she'd have said. It couldn't have anything to do with antique furniture or Fan would have been cultivating his acquaintance like mad on the chance he might be able to do Roger some good.

There was still a chance he might be able to do Holly some good, though. "He told me he was sorry not to see more of you and Roger," she remarked.

"Did he really?" Fan started to put on the Westchester manner she hadn't used for so long, then gave it up with a sigh. "I suppose it wouldn't hurt to ask him over. He'd be somebody for you to know. Though what good it would do—still, if he lent you his library card—"

"Oh, that was just because the librarian was being stuffy

and he heard me tell her I was Roger Howe's sister. What is he: divorced, a widower, or just not interested?"

"A widower, I think. They were saying something once at the Women's Circle about his wife dying young of cancer, but it might have been hearsay. Blast this starter!"

Fan climbed out and lifted the hood. Holly stayed in the cab, opened one of her books, and pretended to read with one eye on the library door. She was glad she'd chosen a biography. It looked intellectual. Ah, here he came, with a book under his arm and both hands in his pockets. Did he look pleased at seeing the truck still there, or was he only amused by the sight of Fan's fuzzy brown behind sticking out from under the hood? Anyway, he wasn't going to pass on without speaking again.

"Having problems, Mrs. Howe? What a bore. Anything I can do?"

"Yes." Fan backed out and stood up to face him. "Find me a halfway reliable second-hand truck, dirt cheap. This heap's about had it. How are you, Professor? Holly was just telling me how you bailed her out with your library card."

"Marie's a stickler for the rules, I'm afraid. What seems to be the problem?"

"Oh, the wiring's all shot. I don't know whether I've made it better or worse. Try the starter again, Holly."

"Where's the key?"

"In my pocket, most likely. Force of habit." Fan wiped her greasy hands on a tattered tissue and fished out the ignition key.

"Here, let me." Cawne took the key from her and slid behind the wheel. To nobody's surprise, the engine purred obediently at his first try.

"There you are, ladies. Not at all. My pleasure."

He smiled away their thanks and gave Fan a gallant boost into the driver's seat. "I do hope I'll have the pleasure of seeing you again while you're here, Miss Howe."

"Come to dinner tonight," Fan said to her own evident

surprise. "Don't ask me what you'll get to eat, but we'll manage something."

"I'm sure it will be delightful." Cawne looked as if he meant it. "What time would you want me?"

"Could you make at quarter to seven? We keep early hours now that we're country folks."

"A quarter to seven is exotically late for Jugtown. My housekeeper will be impressed. See you then."

He waved and turned off toward the shops. Fan put the truck in gear, looking a trifle blank.

"Whatever possessed me to do that? I was planning to go back and get the rest of that paneling. Now we'll have to stay and clean house."

"You go for the boards and I'll do the cleaning," Holly offered, glad of the excuse to dodge another vandalizing expedition. "It'll be good training for my new career."

"You sure do have rotten luck," Fan sympathized in her own fashion. "Just when an interesting man shows up, you go and stick yourself out at Cliff House, where they don't allow visitors."

"Thanks, Fan. You really know how to cheer a person up. What shall I cook for dinner?"

They talked housekeeping the rest of the way back, except for a minor squabble when they passed Cawne's driveway. Holly wanted to turn in for a closer look at the house. Fan was anxious to fix Roger's lunch and hustle herself back to the walnut mine. Fan won.

Chapter 4

"Roger must have a customer!"

Fan got a momentary charge out of seeing an almost-new station wagon parked in the yard. To her chagrin, the visitor turned out not to be a wealthy Yank making a pilgrimage to the master's workshop but Bert's nephew looking for a job.

"That's an expensive car," she fussed. "This Sam must charge a mint for his work. I hope Roger doesn't commit himself to paying so much for the carving that we wind up making zilch out of the furniture. Maybe I'd better go in there."

"Hadn't we better put the groceries away instead?" Holly thought that was more tactful than saying, "Why don't you mind your own business and let Roger mind his?"

Fan brushed her off. "You said you'd do the housework."

So much for tact. Holly picked up two of the grocery bags and lugged them into the house. If Fan chose to barge into the workshop and throw her weight around, that was between her and Roger. What a relief it would be not having to be caught up in this situation twenty-four hours a day.

Claudine needn't have bothered warning her that Cliff House was run down. It couldn't be worse than Howe Hill. The house had never been modernized. Perishables still had to be lugged down to the cellar because there wasn't any fridge. Canned goods and other staples had to be stacked on the pantry shelves because Roger hadn't got around to building cabinets. Oil lamps had to be cleaned and filled, cooking done either on the cranky wood-burning range or else on a frightening little two-burner gasoline camp stove. Holly was trying to get up nerve enough to light it when Fan burst through the back door.

"Holly, he's asked him to lunch! Now what are we going to do?"

"Open another can of soup, that's all. Nobody expects a banquet at lunchtime."

"Jugtowners do. It's breakfast, dinner, and supper up here."

"Then I'll fry some eggs and make hashed browns out of those potatoes left from last night. Light the stove for me, then go fix your face. If they come in before we're ready, I'll offer them whiskey and cheese."

"Roger oughtn't to drink in the daytime. Working with sharp tools—"

"He's a big boy now, Fan. Get cracking, will you?"

Roger this and Roger that. Roger wouldn't take enough whiskey to addle his handsome head and make him cut his little pinkie finger. Too bad Fan hadn't had six or eight kids so she could have spread her maternal urges thin enough to be tolerable. The way she coddled that human haddock was positively scary. Holly slammed a frying pan on the stove, scooped a dollop of marge into the bottom, and started slicing cold boiled potatoes. Whatever had possessed her brother to make such an uncharacteristically spontaneous gesture? This woodcarver must be something special.

Sam Neill didn't look special, nor did he act as if he thought he was. He acknowledged the introduction to Holly pleasantly enough, then seemed quite content to sit down beside the kitchen stove and accept the jelly tumbler of weak whiskey and water with no ice that Holly handed him straight from the sink. He and Roger gnawed absently at hunks of the flavorsome local cheddar she gave them, talking about furniture. Neither of them paid any attention to Holly except to edge out of her way when she had to set the table. No sense in bothering to serve in the dining room. They wouldn't notice.

The men were still talking furniture when they sat down to eat. They talked through the soup, the salad, the eggs and hashed browns, the canned peaches and cookies, the numerous cups of strong tea. Once Neill asked Holly to pass the milk jug. Once he said, "This is very good, Mrs. Howe." Had they been two Chippendale chairs, the two women might have gotten more attention.

Holly didn't mind, she enjoyed listening to them. For the first time since she could remember, she was seeing Roger as a real person, somebody she could be proud of, winning respect from this man who also had the hands, the eyes and the dedication of a master craftsman.

Fan, on the other hand, could take no pleasure in a conversation that left her no chance to talk. She fidgeted, attempted several times to break in, and finally did manage to blurt out, "How much do you expect to get paid, Mr. Neill?"

Holly could tell Neill was shocked and Roger embarrassed, though both of them tried to put a decent face on the matter that should have been handled quietly and offhandedly out in the workshop. Instead Neill was forced to mumble, "Whatever Roger thinks I'm worth," and quickly ask Holly how long she expected to be in Jugtown.

"I don't know yet," she replied. "It depends on how soon I get fired from my new job."

"What job is that?" He was studying her carved-up face with what might have been professional interest.

"I'm a lion tamer. Don't I look it?"

She was sorry as soon as she'd given him the flip reply. Neill was only trying to be polite. "Actually, I've been a photographers' fashion model. There was an accident in the studio when a light broke, and I was injured, as you've no doubt gathered. I'm up here trying to heal. Your uncle mentioned there was an opening at Cliff House for a sort of junior assistant chore girl, so I took it. I may as well be doing something useful, since I'm none too ornamental right now."

"That's about what I'm doing." Neill set down his cup with finality. "Thanks for the dinner."

When he got up from the table, Holly saw he was taller

than she'd realized, almost as tall as Roger and not yet beginning to thicken at the waist. Like so many Maritimers, he had the map of Scotland printed all over his craggy features. His hair and skin had a ruddy glow, his eyes were blue as the bluebonnets over the border, almost as blue as Holly's own. His clothes were what any local workman would wear: a plaid flannel shirt, nondescript trousers, and ankle-high boots with thick soles. He was probably a nice enough chap in his way.

She nodded farewell and began to clear the table. As Neill turned to leave, something about the shape of his back jogged her memory. Then she realized his shirt was the same overall blue color Claudine's anonymous companion had been wearing yesterday.

Fan had noticed, too. "I'll bet you a nickel that's the fellow we saw with Claudine Parlett yesterday," she hissed, casting a wary eye in the direction of the workshop.

Holly poured hot water from the teakettle onto the detergent in the dishpan and sneezed as the bubbles got up her nose. "Gee, that's tough," she said when she could talk.

"What do you mean?"

"Two single people taking an afternoon stroll together doesn't make much of a story, does it?"

"Huh! If that's all they were up to, why couldn't they stroll closer to home? Anyway, how do we know Neill's single? He could have wives all over Canada."

Holly sneezed again. "What fun for him. Them, too, no doubt. Fan, if you intend to get that wood today, you'd better get hopping."

She didn't honestly care whether Fan pulled off another successful raid or if Sam Neill had committed polygamy from sea to shining sea. She only wanted the house to herself. If Howe Hill was to be made even halfway presentable before Geoffrey Cawne arrived, there was no time to be wasted on gossip.

Chapter 5

Getting Howe Hill in order for a party was an uphill fight. Holly swept and dusted, scrubbed and scoured. She conquered the logistics of turning humble fricasseed fowl into glamorous coq au vin, and even managed to bake an apple pie in Fan's unpredictable Dutch oven.

When the two front rooms were as clean as she could get them, Holly went out and picked an armload of the scraggly field asters that were all Howe Hill had to offer by way of flowers, except for the goldenrod she didn't dare bring in because of Roger's allergies. Eked out with branches of maple leaves that had begun to show their fall colors, the arrangements wouldn't look too bad by lamplight.

Maybe she wouldn't, either. With the house and the dinner under reasonable control, Holly lugged hot water up to her bedroom, managed a sponge bath out of a chipped enamel basin, then went to work on her face, using every professional trick she'd ever learned. The result was only fair, so she put on the brightest dress she owned, to call attention away from the damaged areas.

At least Fan was impressed. When she got home from her lumber raid and saw what Holly'd accomplished, she rushed to clean up and change into one of her long-unworn Westchester gowns. The two women went downstairs in grand style, just in time to greet Cawne, who arrived on the dot in great spirits.

"This is an unexpected treat. Who'd have thought I'd be spending my evening with a charming New York hostess and a famous fashion model instead of moaning over a pile of so-

called poems written by future oil-drillers and potato farmers?
Would it be cheeky of me to compliment you on that ravishing
—should I call it a creation, Miss Howe?"

"Call it anything you like, and please call me Holly. How
did you know I'd been a model?"

"I recognized you from your photographs, of course. Surely
you don't think I confine my reading exclusively to the Canadian poets? Are you here on assignment?"

"Hardly." Holly's hands went up to her cheeks. Was he trying to be kind, or making subtle fun of her? "I'm hiding out till
I'm fit to be seen again, if ever," she said bluntly.

"I keep telling Holly the scars aren't half so gruesome as she
thinks they are." Fan did have a knack for choosing her words.

"Scars?" Cawne made a little business of adjusting his
glasses and tilting his head to peer closer at Holly's face. "Oh,
yes, now I see. One just has to squint a bit. I do understand
that in your profession even a minor blemish could seem like a
catastrophe. Were you in an accident?"

Either her camouflage job was better than she'd thought or
the professor needed his glasses changed. In any case, his cool
academic interest was a refreshing change. For the first time
since it had happened, Holly found she didn't mind talking
about her injury.

"It was one of those stupid freak things. A few of us were at
the studio one evening. We'd had a long day's shooting and we
were all a bit punchy, I guess. Anyway, the photographers
were trying different trick shots and I was posing for them,
hoping to get some interesting shots for my portfolio. Somebody was holding two hand floodlamps close to me for a strong
light-and-dark effect. Somebody else got the bright idea of
sloshing water over me to pick up wet highlights. The cold
water hit the hot lamps and"—she spread her hands—"I spent a
month in Bellevue Hospital having slivers of glass picked out
of me."

"Good God! I hope you're suing those idiots for every cent
they've got."

"I can't do that. They're friends of mine."

"I tell her, with friends like them she doesn't need enemies," said Fan. "Sit here, Professor. Roger, why don't you get us some drinks?"

"What will you have, Cawne?"

This was pure swank or gross ignorance on Roger's part. They had nothing in the house but the remains of the whiskey he and Neill had been drinking at lunchtime. Luckily Cawne opted for that. They all settled down around the fireplace that was the house's one redeeming feature. Inevitably the talk turned to antique furniture.

"I must say I envy you, Howe," said their guest, although no sign of discontent showed on his face as he stretched out impeccably trousered legs to the blaze fed with scraps from the workshop. "You're one of the few people I've met who's had the courage to cut loose and do exactly what he wants. I haven't the knowledge to evaluate your work myself, but I believe you're gaining rather a reputation among those who do know. I understand you even use tools of the period."

"Exclusively," said Roger. "I also use a foot-powered lathe dating from the eighteenth century."

Cawne sat up straight, his face aglow. "No! Do you really? I don't suppose you'd allow me to take some photographs of you in your workshop? Er—they'd be for publication, if you'd consent to that."

"Where would they be published?"

The professor smiled and shrugged in Holly's direction. "Nowhere so glamorous as in the fashion magazines, I'm afraid. It would be for a semi-historical work on the preservation of the early arts."

"I hardly qualify as an artist. I am a cabinetmaker. An artisan, if you like."

"Don't be modest, Roger," said his wife impatiently. "You're a real artist. Mrs. Brown said so in her last letter. Mrs. Brown's a famous interior decorator who buys a lot of Roger's things," she explained to Cawne.

"Really?" Their guest looked dutifully impressed. "I hope I meet her sometime. Lecturing in many places as I do, one does run into almost everybody sooner or later. I must say an intimate family party like this makes a delightful change."

He took the last sip of his drink. Before Roger could offer a refill and then have to confess the whiskey was all gone, Holly leaped up.

"Please, Fan, can we sit down now? I'm afraid my chicken will be overcooked."

"I'm sure it will be delicious," said Cawne, willingly following his hostess into the dining room. "What a charming place you have here."

As she and Fan slipped out to get the food, Holly remarked, "Don't you love a guest who's too nearsighted to notice the stains on the wallpaper?" And the scars on one's cheeks. She hadn't felt so cheerful since that bulb exploded.

"Won't it be great if he puts Roger in a book?" Naturally that was all Fan could think of.

Dinner was a great success. Long before dessert was eaten and they'd gone back to the fireplace for coffee, they were all on first-name terms. Holly wouldn't have believed an evening could pass so agreeably at Howe Hill.

"Will you be here long, Holly?" their delightful new friend asked. "I'd love to take you around and show you some of our scenery."

What a rotten break! Why couldn't she have gone to the library before she'd talked to Claudine?

"I'm sorry," she had to tell him. "I've gone and got myself a job."

"Really? I shouldn't think there'd be much call for models around these parts."

"There isn't, I don't suppose. I'm going to be a hired help at Cliff House."

"That will be a change of pace for you, at any rate. Of course it's a tremendous break for me."

Holly gaped at him. "Why do you say that?"

"Because I've gotten permission to take some photographs there for the book I mentioned earlier. Mrs. Parlett's niece was disinclined to let me go in, but Earl Stoodley, the other trustee, talked her down. I have a suspicion Stoodley thinks he's going to get some publicity for his pet project out of it."

Stoodley and a few other people. Holly sneaked a glance at Fan as Geoffrey Cawne went on enthusiastically.

"The point is, Holly, I'm very much an amateur photographer. I've bought all the gadgets and read all the books—well, some of them—but when it comes down to setting up a subject and lighting it properly, I never quite know what to do. Having a professional like you to set me straight would be fantastic. That is, if you wouldn't mind?"

"I'd love it." Holly knew from experience how much preliminary fussing it took to arrange the simplest studio shot. On location, a single photograph could take hours to organize. Being involved with her own field again would be far more fun than mopping floors and changing beds. Working with Geoffrey wouldn't be so bad, either. Her new job was developing some unexpected fringe benefits.

Chapter 6

The next morning Holly stood in front of a half-filled suit-case wondering what to pack next. She hadn't planned to take more than the basic necessities, plus jeans and jerseys and a warm sweater or two. Now that Geoffrey Cawne would be coming to Cliff House, maybe she ought to go prepared with a more intriguing wardrobe.

Then again, maybe she oughtn't. He was too sophisticated a man to be taken in by such an obvious ploy. While she was de-bating the issue, Fan, who'd promised to drive her out to Parlett's Point after breakfast, came pounding up the stairs.

"Hurry, Holly. He's here to pick you up."

"Geoffrey Cawne?"

"Don't you wish it? No, Earl Stoodley, the trustee. He's going to escort you in person."

"Why the fanfare?"

"I told you Cliff House is Earl's big project. He most likely wants to give you a pep talk about guarding the priceless relics. Be nice to him, won't you? There'll surely be some resto-ration needed before they start the museum, and that could be another job for Roger. Come on."

Before Holly could protest that she hadn't finished packing, Fan had grabbed the suitcase, slammed it shut, and chugged away down the stairs, her plump behind waggling in too-tight corduroy pants cut down from an old pair of Roger's. There wasn't much Holly could do but follow. They did manage a quick goodbye before Stoodley hustled her into an elderly

Ford that smelled of fertilizer and began to snake his way back
to the main road.

"It's kind of you to do this, Mr. Stoodley," Holly said, because she thought she ought to.

"Part of my job," he told her with the automatic joviality of
the born politician. "I figured you and I'd better have a little
talk before you got started at Cliff House, eh. I hope you realize what a big responsibility you're taking on. Strictly speaking, Claudine shouldn't have hired you without asking me
first."

"She's awfully worried about Mrs. Parlett."

"Ungh."

Stoodley pursed his babyish lips until they made a small red
dot in the middle of his suety face, like a cherry on top of a
pudding. He was an enormous jelly bag of a man altogether.
"More belly than brains," was how Fan had described him.

Holly wasn't so sure. The shrewdness might be dwarfed by
that ponderous gut, but she could see it gleaming out from the
pale little eyes that kept darting from the road to her face and
back while he primed her with facts about Cliff House and its
role in local history. He was well up on his subject, and talked
with fluency and color. Without coming straight out and saying so, though, he was making it clear Holly needn't fret herself about the two old ladies. Her main responsibility would be
to the house and its furnishings rather than to its bedridden
owner.

"Not much anybody can do for old Mathilde now. She's
lived out her allotted time and then some. You might as well
be prepared for the end to come any day."

And that, she saw, was where Stoodley expected Holly
Howe to fit into the picture. He evidently feared that as soon
as Mrs. Parlett had drawn her last breath, Cliff House would
be overrun by hordes of souvenir hunters, grabbing everything
they could lay their hands on. What he wanted her to do was
simply hang around, make no effort to stave off the fateful mo-

ment, but let him know the instant it happened so that he could rush up and stand guard.

Holly straightened him out fast. "We'd better understand each other right now, Mr. Stoodley. Claudine Parlett hired me to help care for her great-aunt and keep the household running. That's what I plan to do. As a trustee you're naturally entitled to know what's going on, but if you think I'm moving into Cliff House as anybody's paid sneak, you can forget it."

"Now, now, don't get me wrong. I want you to do your job. I only meant—"

"I know what you meant. I'll carry on as best I can, and if anything comes up I think you should know about, I'll give you a call. Let's leave it at that."

Stoodley was too clever to push her any further. He just smiled and tried to pat her knee, but Holly had been a model long enough to develop fast reflexes. The knee wasn't where he patted. He was left making futile motions with a revoltingly dainty hand whose thumb curved backward in a too-supple arc.

"There's another thing we ought to discuss," Holly said, to take his mind off her knee. "Professor Cawne told me he has permission to take photographs at Cliff House. Since I have professional experience in photography, he's asked me to help him. Is that all right?"

"Absolutely." Earl Stoodley nodded into a nest of chins. "That project has my full support. Furthermore, I'll be there myself. The professor asked me to come along and keep an eye on him to make sure he doesn't pinch anything. Geoff's a great kidder, you know."

No, Holly hadn't known. So those cozy sessions she'd been looking forward to were going to be chaperoned by this great tub of lard. She hadn't liked Stoodley before, now she loathed him.

"Yep, Geoff's pretty smart," Stoodley was going on. "If anything should turn up missing when it comes time to settle the estate, nobody will be able to say he took it because I'll be right there watching him."

"And who's going to be watching you?" Holly couldn't resist asking.

"Why, you are," said Stoodley.

So that was it. Stoodley was a fox and she was a fool. Now if valuables were lost, he'd have Holly Howe to lay the blame on.

"Mr. Stoodley," she said, "I'd like to know whether a complete inventory has been taken at Cliff House. If not, I suggest you turn straight around and drive me back to Howe Hill."

The man beamed as though she'd said something witty. "You've got a long head on those young shoulders. Rest easy, Holly. First thing after I was appointed trustee, the lawyer and I came out here and listed everything from the parlor chesterfield to Jonathan Parlett's false teeth that his wife still kept in a tumbler beside the bed, don't ask me why. Got used to seeing them there, I suppose. Mathilde had got so she wouldn't throw away so much as an empty cracker box, so the inventory was an awful job. I could have used Claudine's help, but she wouldn't come. Trust a woman to hold a grudge. Anyway, it's all written down and filed in a tin box at the lawyer's office, so you don't have a thing to worry about."

"Oh don't I?" Holly thought, but it was too late to back out now. They'd reached Cliff House. She could see a wizened face through the window, pushing aside a grimy lace curtain and peering through smeared glass. That must be the housekeeper, Annie Blodgett. No wonder Claudine worried about her being able to carry on alone. Annie looked almost as old as the house itself.

Cliff House was an enormous square of gray clapboard and garish stained glass, with a slate roof and a whole row of fancy wrought-iron lightning rods at the peak. Its little front porch looked like the observation platform on an old-fashioned train, with a totally useless iron fence around the roof.

Maybe the porch was meant to be symbolic. Stoodley had told her the Parlett fortune came from manufacturing plumbing fixtures for Pullman cars. She'd taken that as a hopeful omen. Cliff House might even have indoor plumbing and a real bathtub. That would be a pleasant change from Howe Hill.

After Stoodley stopped the car, Holly got out her suitcase and went up the steps trying to smile, hoping her facial scars wouldn't scare off that already frightened-looking old housekeeper. Apparently they didn't. She could hear bolts being drawn and chains rattling. Holly expected the hinges to creak when the massive oak door at last swung open, and they did.

"Morning, Annie," said Stoodley. "I expect Claudine phoned you about our new girl here?"

"Yes, and I sure am glad you've come, Helen. Was it Helen she told me? I wrote your name down somewhere, but I can't seem to—" Annie fluttered into silence, wiping a veined claw across her wrinkled chin.

"I'm Holly," said the new girl. "You may know my brother Roger Howe, the cabinetmaker."

"The one Bert works for?" Annie brightened up. "Bert talks about your folks a blue streak, but I've never met them. I don't get out."

"Maybe you'll be able to take some time off now that I'm here."

Holly sounded false and hearty, like Earl Stoodley. She couldn't help it. Inside, the gloom, dust, and clutter were enough to depress anybody. And this was only the front hall. What must the rest of Cliff House be like?

Annie didn't seem to know how to cope with the situation. She dithered back and forth across the doorsill until Stoodley had to ask, "How about it, Annie? Going to let us in?"

"Oh Earl, I don't know."

"Why not? Claudine says it's all right."

"Claudine's never heard what I have. It was here again last night, Earl."

Holly had to lean forward to catch the end of the sentence. The housekeeper's voice had sunk to a terrified whisper.

"Now, Annie." Stoodley gave Holly a knowing wink. "Old houses always squeak and groan at night."

"I know this house a long sight better than you do, Earl Stoodley." Annie might be scared, but there was still a little fight left in her. "Why in Heaven's name won't anybody believe me?"

"There, there. Don't you start taking on." The trustee's tone was like baby oil, soothing and greasy. "I'm not saying I don't believe you. Why shouldn't Jonathan Parlett's ghost come back and haunt his own house if it takes a notion? What ghost's got a better right, eh?" He winked at Holly again.

"Maybe he's after his teeth," Holly giggled. She couldn't help it. A terrified old housekeeper in a mouldering mansion set on a lonely spit of land overlooking this great bay with its menacing tides was too totally stage gothic. Maybe Annie and Stoodley had worked out this act together, as publicity for the museum-to-be. More likely, isolation and overwork had worn poor Annie's nerves to the breaking point and beyond. Holly slipped a comforting arm around the humped shoulders.

"We're going to manage just fine. I'm not afraid of ghosts and you won't be either, now that I'm here to keep you company. Where do you want me to sleep?"

"Cousin Edith's room is the nicest, but that was where—"

"Cousin Edith's room will be fine. I presume Cousin Edith isn't around any more?"

"Not that I know of. We buried her forty years ago, or was it forty-five? My poor head's got so it won't hold a thing."

"Never mind," said Stoodley. "You go on up and get Holly's room ready. I want to show her the front parlor."

He beckoned Holly into the huge room and shut the door. "I guess I don't have to draw you a picture," he murmured.

"You certainly don't," she snapped back. "Now I see why Claudine Parlett's been so worried. It's too bad nobody else is interested in Mrs. Parlett as well as her possessions."

For once, Stoodley had nothing to say. Holly brushed past him, got her suitcase from the front hall, and went up the grand staircase, her feet driving puffs of dust out of the heavy carpeting at every step. By the time she'd reached the second floor, she'd built up a gigantic sneeze. Unfortunately, it exploded just as she came to where Annie Blodgett was leaning over a bed, feeling to see if the mattress was damp. The old woman jumped and turned dead-white.

"My stars!" she gasped. "You scared me out of a year's growth."

"I'm sorry, I had dust up my nose."

Holly felt like a worm. Jonathan Parlett's ghost mightn't be real, but Annie's terror certainly was. No wonder. The atmosphere around here was enough to give anybody the jimjams. She hoped Cliff House owned a vacuum cleaner. As soon as Stoodley got out from under foot, she was going to do something about that dust.

The house was worth cleaning. Spruced up and redecorated, it could easily become the showplace Stoodley dreamed of.

According to the brief historical sketch Geoffrey Cawne had given her last night, the Parletts had been Loyalists from Boston who'd fled to Canada at the first sign of revolution. They'd loaded a coasting vessel with all their household possessions and sailed up here with every chattel intact. They'd built a log cabin here at Parlett's Point, lived in it until they could erect a frame house nearby, raised a few more generations of Parletts, then finally built the present place and torn down the older houses for firewood.

Cawne seemed to think it a pity that the Parletts had kept on making money down through the years. If they'd been less successful, the frame house or even the log cabin might still be here. Though less rich in historical interest, this third and last house did have its own importance. Its dust-covered accumulations were a record of one family's survival from century to century, a long strand in the tapestry of Canada's history.

And now Cliff House was going out of Parlett hands. How did Claudine and her brother feel about that? Was the feud with Mrs. Parlett caused by her having willed Cliff House to the town, or had old Mathilde made that strange will as a result of the quarrel? Annie Blodgett must know and would probably tell, once they could get cozied down by themselves over a cup of tea.

Her curiosity could keep. Right now Cousin Edith's room had to be cleaned and aired. Holly wasn't about to sleep under a canopy of cobwebs. "Annie," she asked, "where do you keep the cleaning stuff?"

"Eh? Oh, downstairs in the broom closet beside the back stairwell." Annie emitted an apologetic titter as she led Holly down the back stairs. "I daresay you don't think much of my housekeeping, but one pair of hands can do just so much work, as I've told Claudine time and again."

Blessedly, there was a vacuum cleaner, a cumbersome black upright that would make a good exhibit for the museum. It worked, though, and made enough noise to drown out whatever Earl Stoodley was trying to get off his chest. The trustee hung around for a while to show he was still in charge, then gave up and took off.

As soon as Annie had put up the chains and bolts after him, Holly shut off the machine. "I hope this racket isn't disturbing Mrs. Parlett," she said.

"No, dearie. Mrs. Parlett doesn't seem to notice noises any more. It's awful to see her lying there so shriveled up and helpless. She was a fine figure of a woman in her day. Wouldn't you like a nice cup of tea?"

"Later, thanks."

Holly was beginning to understand how Cliff House had got so filthy. How could anybody clean around this clutter of highboys and lowboys and chairs and tables and bundles of old magazines and rolled-oats boxes full of buttons and screws and twists of string? She had all she could do to maneuver a path among them, especially with Annie right there tripping over the cord and shrieking snatches of information into her ear.

". . . brought over from London the time Eleazer Parlett went to see the king. George the Second that was, or maybe

George the Third. Earl would know. Anyway, it came up on the ship at the time of the trouble. You'd never think a dainty little thing like that could have survived all these years."

"No, you wouldn't." Holly shut off the Hoover again so she could pay respectful attention where it was surely due. This small, round table with its exquisite pierced gallery was in an amazing state of preservation, considering its drama-crowded history. To have been tossed and churned across the Atlantic two centuries ago in a sailing ship, to be snatched from under the noses of Sam Adams and John Hancock and brought up here to the wilderness, to be pickled in smoke from a crude fieldstone fireplace, chilled by winds howling in between mud-chinked logs; to have been moved from house to house amid generations of growing children; finally to be subjected to the kind of neglect Holly saw all around her, and still not show so much as a scratch, a nick, or a time crack was almost incredible. What wouldn't Roger give to have this table as a model?

Come to think of it, hadn't her brother finished a similar table recently? Holly vaguely recalled being dragged out to the workshop the day she'd arrived from New York, still bandaged and in great pain, to admire a piece that was ready to be shipped to Mrs. Brown.

She closed her eyes, trying to visualize the piece she'd seen once by the light of a kerosene lantern, standing proudly on Roger's workbench surrounded by tins of wax and greasy rubbing cloths. The total design couldn't possibly have been the same, but the shape and proportions were surely similar. Maybe she could get Geoffrey to take this one's picture, or she might wheedle the original sketches out of Fan for comparison. Mrs. Brown always demanded that her sketches and descriptive notes be returned with the finished pieces, no doubt because she was afraid Roger might make a second copy for another customer. They were duly sent back to New York. Little did Mrs. Brown know, though, that Fan always made Xeroxes first, and put the copies in that scrapbook she was keeping to write her memoirs with.

Anyway, the little table must be a favorite of Annie's since it appeared to be one of the few pieces that ever got dusted. It was filmed with gray, but there was no buildup of grime around that little gallery. When Holly flipped a dustrag across the top, its luster came up like magic. If she hadn't known better, she'd have sworn the piece was brand-new.

Holly gave the priceless relic a last, reverent wipe and went on with her noisy task. She blasted a clean path through the hallway and up the stairs, got her own room in passable shape, and was back at the vacuuming when Annie came to tell her dinner was ready. She ate soggy fried potatoes and leathery fried eggs, decided she'd have to become cook as well as charwoman, and went back to work.

By late afternoon Holly was aching all over, filthy from hair to sneakers, and barely able to breathe because her nostrils were so clogged with dust. Her last job of the day was to scour the zinc-lined bathtub so she could take the first good, long, hot soak she'd had since the day she was hurt.

Chapter 7

Holly stayed in the tub until the water cooled off, loving every second of it. At last she struggled out over the varnished wood casing and dried herself on a yellowed but sumptuous towel monogrammed M. For Mathilde, no doubt, poor soul.

Getting dressed again was too much bother for the short time she intended to stay up after supper. Holly put on a warm nightgown and a long zippered robe patterned in blue, green, and purple. Its high mandarin neckline and knuckle-length sleeves ought to satisfy whatever notions of propriety Annie Blodgett might have, and it would be warm to sit around in.

Now that she wasn't pushing the Hoover around, Holly could feel the chill that pervaded Cliff House. Luckily she'd packed a pair of fleece-lined blue-leather house boots, so she put them on, too. Then she remembered Bert Walker might be around doing chores and added some silver jewelry to make the robe look less bedroomy.

It was as well she did. When she got downstairs, she found Bert sitting in front of the stove with his boots off and his feet stuck in the oven to warm. A noisome pipe was in his mouth and a tumbler of hot whiskey and water in his hand. From the quantity of potatoes Annie was peeling, Holly deduced Bert would be staying to supper. He took the pipe out of his mouth and gave her a friendly greeting, but didn't get up to find her a chair.

Annie laid down the paring knife and shook her hands free of potato peelings so she could adjust her spectacles for a better look. "Now don't you look pert! All dressed up and no place to go, eh? Too bad we don't have a nice young man around."

"Bert's nice enough for me," Holly answered. "I only wore this thing because it's warm. Shall I finish the potatoes?"

"No, dearie, you sit still and rest your pretty bones. I tell you, Bert Walker, I never saw anybody work the way this young woman did today. She went through this place like a dose of salts."

"Annie, I hardly scraped the surface."

Holly disclaimed the praise, but didn't need coaxing to collapse into one of the kitchen chairs. She wouldn't have minded sticking her throbbing leg up near the warm oven, too, but the emanations from Bert's gently simmering socks were too powerful.

It was comfortable here in the kitchen, now that the smell of cooking was beginning to overcome the aroma of Bert's feet. The two old cronies kept up a pleasantly monotonous stream of conversation that was restful after Fan's eternal, strident bids for attention and Roger's chilly politeness. The good wood fire in the big iron stove made the room feel cozy. Both the varnished linoleum on the floor and the checkered oilcloth on the table could have done with a scrubbing, but on the whole, the kitchen was in more tolerable order than any other place in the house except Mathilde Parlett's bedroom.

Holly had peeked in while she was vacuuming the upstairs hallway and seen the mistress of Cliff House, wrinkled and brown, tiny as an apple-head doll, her few wisps of white hair straggling over an immaculate linen pillow slip with a heavy crocheted lace edge. The bed she lay on had tall, gracefully fluted posts surmounted by miniature carved pineapples. That piece had reminded Holly of another picture in Fan's scrapbook. Naturally enough, she supposed. Antique reproductions were supposed to look like real antiques.

Supper was eatable, though not by a wide margin. Flustered by so much companionship and a hot toddy she'd taken to steady her nerves, Annie had let the potatoes scorch and the slices of warmed-over beef frizzle to shoe leather. The pickles were good, though. Holly ate a lot of pickles and not much of the rest.

Bert polished off everything in sight, then said reverently, "Thank God for that bite. Many a poor man could have made a meal of it. What else have you got, Annie?"

"I meant to make a pie in Holly's honor, but somehow I never got around to it. You'll have to make do with 'lasses cake."

"Suits me."

Bert accepted a hunk the size and heft of a double-bitted axe head and washed it down with tea strong enough to float the whole axe. Holly cut herself a ladylike sliver, then wished she hadn't been so dainty. Annie's molasses cake was marvelous. She'd know better next time.

Funny, she was already feeling more at home with these two likable old boozers than she'd ever felt anywhere before. What was going to happen to them when the woman upstairs died, as she soon must? Would Earl Stoodley let Annie and Bert stay on as custodians? After that sterling performance she'd put on with the antique Hoover, maybe he'd consider Holly for the job of permanent charlady. She smiled at the thought, and Bert caught her.

"What's so funny, young woman?"

"Nothing, really. I'm just enjoying myself. You're a couple of real fun kids, in case you didn't know it."

"Isn't she sweet?" Annie shed a few alcoholic tears and patted her new helper's somewhat toilworn hand. "Oh dearie, it's going to be just lovely having you here."

"Ayuh," said Bert. "Well, I better stir my stumps. Sam will be up here any time now."

Annie hopped up. "Bert, you never told me Sam was coming. Land's sake, I'd better boil up a fresh kettle."

"Don't bust your garters, woman. Sam's comin' to pick me up, that's all. I left the truck so's Lorraine could cart a bunch o' junk over to the church for some fool flea market they're havin'. Why anybody would pay for a mess o' fleas when they can get all they want for nothin' is beyond me. I told 'er so, but she wouldn't listen. Women never do."

"I s'pose you think you're being funny. Well, I better get up and wash the dishes." Annie leaned back in the rocking chair and closed her eyes.

Holly took the hint. "I'll do them. You cooked the supper."

Annie's only reply was a gentle snore. Holly filled the dishpan, enjoying the luxury of hot water straight from the faucet, found an incongruous plastic squeeze bottle of pink detergent among the ancient milk strainers and bootjacks in the cupboard under the sink, and set to work. As she sudsed and rinsed, Bert came and went a few times, clattering logs into the woodbox beside the big iron stove with no concern about waking his lady friend. Then he disappeared, perhaps to cut more wood.

Holly finished the dishes, cleaned out the sink, and was giving the table top the scouring it so badly needed when a head poked around the outside door.

"Hey, Bert?"

She jumped. "Oh, it's you, Mr. Neill. Bert's around back somewhere, I think. Won't you—" she stopped just in time, remembering Claudine's orders about not letting anybody into the house.

The woodcarver must have known the rules. "I'd better not," he said. "Why don't you come out?"

Holly started to say, "I'm not dressed," then didn't. She was a lot more dressed than she'd been in some of the bathing-suit photos she'd posed for. Anyway, Neill wouldn't have any ideas about roaming in the gloaming since he'd only come to collect his uncle. She picked up a black knitted shawl that was lying across an iron cot in the far corner of the kitchen, draped it around her, and stepped outside.

"Watch out for that broken step. Bert ought to fix it." Sam Neill reached out a helping hand in a friendly way Holly rather liked. "You don't look much like a hired girl in that outfit."

"Is that a compliment or a criticism?"

"Just an observation. I don't know anything about women's clothes."

"Too bad I'm not a Sheraton highboy. You might find me a more interesting study."

Neill grinned. "Lay off, will you? I've had enough Sheraton to last me awhile."

"I thought you and Roger were two hearts that beat as one."

"Did you?" The woodcarver picked up a twig and gave it an expert's appraisal before he threw it away. "He knows his stuff."

"I suppose he does." Holly pulled the shawl tighter. The air was sharper now that the sun had begun to sink. "Frankly, I find this whole Jugtown scene rather incredible. Roger was always my big brother, the banker."

"So Bert was telling me. He quit a high-powered job in New York and sold his fancy estate to come up to the old homestead and do his thing. Quite a story."

"I'm sure Bert made it sound like one. Actually Roger was only a junior trust officer or something and the house was a nice enough split-level in an okay suburb. Roger had a workshop in the basement there, but I'd never realized he did much more than putter. Of course, I didn't know him all that well."

"Seems funny, not knowing your own brother."

"I suppose it does," Holly admitted, "but that's the way it was. Still is, for that matter. Oh, look!"

The sun was slipping into the bay, creating a giant spread of gold and pearl spiked with screaming salmon-pink. Standing here on this high terrace with the hillside sloping down to the cliffs that rimmed Parlett's Point, Holly felt as if she could reach out and grab the sunset, and wear it for a scarf.

"This is nothing," said Neill. "You ought to be up in the Northwest Territory sometime when the aurora borealis starts bouncing off a few thousand acres of snow and ice. Ma Nature's a gaudy old floozie when she gets dolled up."

Neill spoke with offhand affection, as though the earth spirit was one of those many wives Fan had thought up for him. Holly began to wonder about this chap who'd looked so commonplace back in the kitchen at Howe Hill. He could have been Claudine's companion in the woods, at that. Even standing a few feet away from him, she could feel something that made her want either to edge away or move nearer. She escaped into small talk.

"Are you really interested in doing what Roger does?"

"No!" His reaction was explosive. "Slavishly reproducing other people's designs would drive me out of my skull if I had to stick at it for long. Your brother's really got the bug, though. I tried to show him how the design of that highboy could be improved by a slight modification in a curve, and I honestly thought he was going to come after me with a chisel."

"Roger would never do that," said Holly. "He'd just freeze you with that cold politeness of his. I've wondered whether Roger makes such a fetish of authenticity because he hasn't the talent to do original work."

"Some people are more comfortable following a set pattern. Howe's a superb craftsman at any rate. Furthermore, you have to respect his courage about doing what feels right to him. Here's Bert coming. You going to be around tomorrow night?"

He slipped in the question so casually that Holly almost said yes without thinking. Did this backwoods Romeo expect her to be panting on the doorstep?

"I'll be here," she told him, "but I can't say whether I'll be free. Professor Cawne's going to be doing some photography in the house for a book he's writing, and I've been asked to help him. I don't know how long it will take."

"Oh, Cawne's a pretty fast worker, I'd say."

Neill shrugged and went over to his station wagon. Holly stepped back inside, wondering why she felt so annoyed with herself for having said what was so obviously the right thing to say.

Chapter 8

By that time, Holly was ready to call it a day. Annie wasn't. Refreshed by her nap and the excitement of having someone to talk to, she appeared ready to make a night of it. She reminisced about her years at Cliff House until Holly could no longer hide her yawns.

"I'm sorry, Annie, but I've got to get some sleep."

"I expect we should both go to bed," Annie sighed. "I can't say I relish the notion."

"Why not?"

The old woman lifted a stove lid, poked at dull red embers with the cast-iron lifter, thrust in two more chunks of hardwood, fiddled with the dampers. "There, I guess that ought to hold overnight. We used to burn coal, but Earl Stoodley's too cheap to buy us any these days. I do hate coming down to a cold stove in the morning when my tongue's hanging out for a good, hot cup of tea. Don't you?"

She took off her dirty apron and hung it with exaggerated care on a hook behind the pantry door while Holly waited, none too patiently. At last Annie wiped her palms down the front of her faded print dress and confessed, "The plain truth of the matter is, I'm scared."

"Because of those noises you were talking about to Mr. Stoodley? You don't honestly believe it's ghosts, do you?"

"Dearie, I don't know what to believe, and that's the God's honest truth. I don't imagine those noises. I hear them as plain as I can hear that pretty voice of yours, and you needn't start reminding me everybody hears funny sounds at night in old houses. I've lived in this house long enough to know every squeak and groan it's ever made. These noises are different."

"How different?"

"The best I can describe it is like somebody padding around in shoepacs or moccasins. Sometimes I hear them downstairs, sometimes up attic, sometimes it seems to be right in the room next to where I'm lying. Sometimes it's just the footsteps I hear, other times it's bumping noises like furniture being moved around."

Holly raised her eyebrows. "You don't suppose it could be ordinary flesh-and-blood burglars?"

"Dearie, I may be an old fool but I'm not a damn fool, as Bert would say. Naturally that was the first thing I thought of. But when I get up the next morning and check around, everything's the same as I left it the night before. I've got Earl Stoodley up here with that inventory list of his more than once, and nothing's ever been missing far's we can make out. The doors and windows are always locked. I've gone around to every crack and cranny, but there's never any sign of breaking in, and why should anybody do that anyway if it wasn't to steal? So, if it isn't ghosts, what is it, eh?"

"I don't know, Annie." Holly yawned again. "But whatever it is, I'll hear it too, and we can compare notes in the morning."

"But it might not happen tonight. Sometimes weeks go by and I don't hear anything out of the ordinary. Lately it's been coming more often, though. I couldn't tell you how many times I've gone down those stairs with a poker in my fist and my heart in my mouth."

"You mean you've actually gone chasing after the sounds?"

"Of course, dearie. I'm not that much of a coward. What scares me most of all is when I can't. Nowadays it seems every time I hear something and try to get out, the door to my bedroom sticks shut. It's like those nightmares where somebody's chasing after you and you can't budge hand or foot. Yet the door isn't locked because I keep the key. And the next morning I can open it easily enough. It's as if there's a spell on it."

"Do you normally sleep with your door shut?"

"Always, ever since I came here. Aunt Maude made me. She was afraid Uncle Jonathan might be going to the bathroom in his nightshirt, see, and it wouldn't be nice if I should happen to wake up and see him."

"Who was Aunt Maude? I thought Mrs. Parlett's name was Mathilde."

"Uncle Jonathan married twice. Aunt Maude was the first. She wasn't really my aunt, just my mother's cousin, but it sounded more respectful to call her Aunt Maude. Anyway, as I say, I always shut my door but I never used to lock it. You can bet your bottom dollar I do now, though it doesn't seem to matter one way or the other. I hang the key on a string around my neck because they say iron's a charm against witches. Laugh if you want to."

"I'm not laughing," said Holly. Annie Blodgett might be a naïve country woman, but she certainly had her wits about her. "And you say nothing is ever moved or taken away?"

"Never once. I'll admit my eyes aren't what they used to be, but I've got Earl and his inventory to back me up. He'd squawk fast enough if he found anything missing. No dearie, the only explanation that makes sense to me is a ghost. I don't know if it's Uncle Jonathan or Aunt Maude or Cousin Edith or who, but I say it's a Parlett."

"What does Bert say?"

"Nothing much I'd care to repeat," Annie answered primly, "but he's as stumped as I am."

"And Claudine?"

"Tells me to say my prayers and keep my door locked, as if I needed to be told."

"Then they both—" Holly hesitated, not sure how to go on without hurting Annie's feelings.

"They don't think I'm dreaming, the way Earl Stoodley does, if that's what you're driving at. They know me, you see."

Holly nodded. She understood now why both Bert and Claudine had shown such a peculiar mixture of eagerness and hesitation about finding a companion for Annie. She ought to resent being put on the spot like this, but she didn't. For once, she was finding herself needed as a responsive human being instead of merely a prop to dress a stage or focus a lens on. She gave Annie a little hug.

"If it's one of the Parletts, you shouldn't have to worry about coming to any harm. You've done plenty for them over the years, haven't you?"

"I've done the best I could, dearie, and I'll keep on as long as the Lord spares me and the family needs me."

They got to bed at last. Annie must have passed a peaceful night, for Holly never got waked up. She slept until almost eight o'clock, but the extra sleep left her surprisingly unrefreshed. Annie, on the other hand, was chipper as a sparrow.

"That's the first decent night's rest I've had since I can remember when. Set yourself down, dearie, and let me fix you a nice bowl of porridge. I've already fed Mrs. Parlett."

Holly shuddered at the lumpy, gluey gray mass Annie was offering. "Thanks, but I'd rather have toast and a boiled egg, if we have any."

"Land, yes, eggs enough to start our own henyard. They're in that brown crockery bowl in the pantry."

She started to go for the eggs but Holly stopped her. "I'll do it, Annie. You shouldn't be waiting on me. I meant to be down in time to cook breakfast for you."

"Ah, it takes an old fox to beat a young chicken," Annie bubbled. "You sure you won't have any porridge? You young things, always fussing about your figures! When I was a girl, boys liked a girl with a waist they could really get hold of. Land alive! Aunt Maude must be rolling over in her grave, me saying a thing like that. Anyway, dearie, you'd better eat hearty. We've a big day ahead of us."

"Why? What's happening?"

"Professor Cawne telephoned just a little while before you came down. He's coming out here with Earl Stoodley to take pictures, and he says you're going to be in on it."

Holly dropped her egg into the pan too quickly and cracked

the shell. "Blast! Yes, I did promise to help but I thought he'd give me a day or so to get squared away first. I don't know what shots he's planning to take, what he wants for props or backgrounds—"

Since Annie didn't have the faintest idea what she was talking about and since she couldn't do anything now anyway except muddle through, Holly quit sputtering and concentrated on making toast the way Annie showed her. You speared a slice of bread with a long fork, lifted a stove lid, and held the bread close to the shimmering red embers just long enough, but not too long or you'd wind up with charcoal. It was remarkably good toast, when you managed it right. Holly was working on her third slice when Earl Stoodley's Ford and Geoffrey Cawne's gray Jaguar swished up to the front portico.

Both men jumped out and started lugging in a great deal of equipment. Stoodley tripped over the leg of a tripod and almost went flying on his fat face. That brightened Holly's morning a little. Puttering around with things she knew and understood was fun, too, even with Earl making inane comments and the floodlights giving her the creeps every time she got too close to one.

Geoffrey Cawne hadn't just been modest about calling himself an amateur with a camera, she found. He didn't know the first thing about rigging reflectors to eliminate shadows or other technicalities.

Holly tried to persuade him that the little galleried table would be a good subject to start on, both because of its historical interest and because it was small enough to give few problems photographically. Like a typical amateur, though, Geoffrey set his heart on an immense armoire that stood in a next-to-impossible location, was too heavy to move, and had stacks of assorted junk piled in front of it. They spent half the morning just clearing away debris, sweeping the floor, dusting and polishing the armoire, and draping a white bedsheet behind it to provide a less distracting background than the dismal, stained wallpaper.

Earl Stoodley toiled gamely, keeping up a brave pretense of knowing what the activity was all about. Annie Blodgett hovered wherever she'd be most in the way chirping, "When are you going to take the picture?" over and over like an elderly parakeet until Holly shooed her away to make them all a nice cup of tea. She for one desperately needed it.

Then they had to drink the tea. Then they had to focus the camera. Then they had to figure out why Geoffrey's expensive strobe flash wouldn't go off when it was supposed to. Then at last they took the picture.

Once he'd got rolling, Geoffrey took a great many exposures: with the cabinet doors closed, with them open, with one open and the other shut, then the closed door open and the open one shut. He shot from the front, the right, the left, from a high angle, from a low angle. Annie wondered how many pictures of that old wardrobe he was going to put in his book, for the land's sake.

"One," Cawne replied cheerfully.

"Then why in tarnation didn't you take just one?"

"That's not how it's done," Earl Stoodley told her.

"Cat's foot, Earl! You know no more about it than I do."

Annie was really perking this morning, no more the cringing little crone who'd peered so timorously at them through the curtains only a day ago.

"Earl's right, Mrs. Blodgett," said Cawne. "The idea is to take a great many different pictures, then pick out the one that shows the subject to best advantage. That's how professional photographers work. Right, Holly?"

"Absolutely. Sometimes they may take as many as thirty or forty shots just to get one that's right in every way. We're not doing too badly on shooting time compared to some sessions I've been involved with. Of course a lot of the time the model's just sitting around trying not to chew her fingernails no matter how frustrated she gets."

She held out grubby hands with two nails already broken

off. "Good thing I've retired from modeling, or you'd have to find yourself another prop girl."

"I'd hate that." Geoffrey's smile was worth the loss of a few fingernails.

By now it was well past noon. Holly expected Annie to offer the men a bite to eat but she didn't, not even when Earl started croaking about how his stomach told him it was dinner-time.

"So it is," said Cawne in apparent surprise. "I must get along or my housekeeper will be annoyed. Is there any chance of coming back and taking another shot or two this afternoon, do you think?"

"You come right ahead, Professor," Stoodley took it upon himself to answer. "And Holly, you help him like you been doing. This is more important than running that old Hoover. We'll have to bring in a professional cleaning crew anyway."

When Mrs. Parlett died, he meant. At least he had sense enough not to say so. The men went away, leaving their equipment strewn around, and the women turned toward the kitchen.

"Annie, why didn't you offer to fix them a sandwich or something?" Holly asked her.

"And have Earl Stoodley throw it up to me forever after about feeding outsiders at the estate's expense, even if it was himself that ate the grub? You don't know Earl the way I do, dearie. I don't know's I'd go so far as to call him dishonest, but I sure wouldn't trust him to sell me a horse, as Uncle Jonathan used to say. Not that I'm in the market for one, or ever will be. What do you want for dinner?"

"What's on the menu? By the way, how do we manage about groceries?"

"Claudine phones once or twice a week and asks what I need. Then she gets it and either Earl or Bert brings up the bundles. That's one reason I have to watch my step. Earl knows to a penny what we spend on food here, and don't think he's above prying around in the pantry to make sure I haven't snuck in an extra can of beans."

"How do you account for what Bert Walker eats?"

"Why should I have to? Bert's hired help, same as you or me. Jonathan Parlett never begrudged a decent meal to anybody that worked for him and neither will I, long as I'm running this kitchen. I told Earl Stoodley so to his face, and I guess Claudine must have stuck up for me because I never heard any more about that. We might as well open a can of chicken soup. I can always get that down Mrs. Parlett with no trouble. Chicken's her favorite, Claudine says. I get sick and tired of it, myself."

"Then why don't you ask Claudine to buy something else for a change? How does Claudine know what Mrs. Parlett likes anyway, if they've been on the outs all this time?"

"Now dearie, don't you go blaming Claudine. It's not easy for her."

"Then why doesn't she make it easier? If Claudine's so concerned about her great-aunt, I can't for the life of me understand why she never comes to see her."

"Claudine would never do that!"

Annie sounded so upset that Holly dropped the subject and sat down to her chicken soup. Didn't they ever have salads or fresh fruit at Cliff House? She'd have to try a little diplomacy about the shopping list when Earl Stoodley came back for the afternoon's photography session.

Chapter 9

To her surprise, Cawne returned alone. "Why, Geoffrey," Holly exclaimed, "what happened to our beloved trustee?"

"Earl found he had pressing business elsewhere. I suspect he's become disenchanted with the glamorous world of photography. I hope you're not?"

"Oh no, I'm still enchanted as anything. What shall we do next?"

"Stoodley tells me there's a wig stand on which a distant relative of Queen Anne once parked his peruke. That sounds intriguing, don't you think? Could Mrs. Blodgett find it for us?"

"I expect so. She's upstairs right now, giving Mrs. Parlett her back rub. I'll go and ask."

"No, Holly, please don't leave me alone."

"Why not? Don't tell me you're afraid of the ghost?"

"No, I'm afraid of Stoodley, to be honest. He's terrified of losing his prize exhibits, and I don't want anyone ever to say I was given the chance to pinch something. I'm sure he phoned here as soon as he got home, to give you dire warnings against letting me roam about on my own."

"Nothing of the sort," said Holly. "He did give me a strong warning against letting people into the house and so did Claudine Parlett, but Earl says you're to have all the help you want. You must be on his top security clearance list."

"Well, well!" Cawne found that idea vastly amusing. "If Stoodley knew what a jungle the groves of academe can be, he'd think twice about turning me loose in here. Be that as it may, I'd still rather you stayed close to me. For more reasons than one, if I dare say so."

Holly wasn't sure how to take that. "So that while I'm watching you, you can keep an eye on me? Maybe Earl Stoodley's been talking to you, too."

"I assure you he hasn't."

Cawne looked so discomfited that Holly apologized. "I'm sorry. It's just that I didn't realize what I was taking on till I got here. I thought Cliff House would be full of mustache cups and antimacassars. Instead, here's all this priceless stuff. It's scary."

"I can see it would be," he agreed. "For me their value is in their historical associations, but I know some people do pay tremendous sums for the dubious privilege of owning pieces that ought to be in public museums. Well, since we have to wait for the wig stand, what shall we do to fill the time? I'll let you pick one."

"How about this Bible box? See how well it's preserved?"

"If you say so." Cawne didn't act thrilled by her choice, though he started loading his camera while Holly set up the shot.

"Would it be too hokey to set a candlestick next to the Bible box and maybe lay a pair of those tiny Ben Franklin spectacles on the table? I think there's a pair in the back parlor. We could go together to look for them," she couldn't resist adding.

"So we could, like Jack and Jill. I'm rather up on nursery rhymes. One of my young lady students did a paper on Mother Goose. Your idea sounds delightful. What we need is a pewter candlestick. Is there one about, do you know?"

There wasn't, only fancy Victorian wrought-iron affairs that Geoffrey said wouldn't do at all. They settled for a squat green glass inkwell with a somewhat moth-eaten turkey quill stuck into the neck. The feather's vertical arc would break up the austere squareness of the box.

Holly fussed with her props, taking out the huge leather-bound Bible and opening it to the pages where births and deaths had been recorded down through the generations. The inkstand could suggest somebody was about to add a new leaf to the family tree.

But there'd never be any more babies at Cliff House. Soon Earl Stoodley would be happily scrawling "Died" after Mrs. Parlett's name, and that would be that. She wished she'd picked a different subject.

Geoffrey must have wished so, too. He was polite about her arrangement but wasted little film on the shot. After a couple of exposures, he asked, "What next?"

Holly couldn't help feeling dashed. "Aren't you going to take any with the lid open?"

"I don't see why. There's nothing interesting about the inside."

But there was. As Holly raised the lid to put the Bible back in, she noticed a little stain on the wood, shaped exactly like a swimming duck. She slammed down the lid, praying Geoffrey wouldn't notice her hands were shaking. Now she knew why the box was in such a remarkable state of preservation. That stain was her own blood.

It had happened the first time Fan had dragged her along on a lumber raid. In wrenching a board loose, Holly had slashed her finger painfully. She'd got no sympathy.

"Don't bleed on the wood," Fan had screamed. "The stain will never come out."

The warning had come too late. A drop had already fallen on the dried-out board. Holly remembered how she'd stood appalled, watching the blood spread into that oddly whimsical shape while Fan railed at her.

"Now see what you've done! Roger will have a fit."

He'd been none too happy, at any rate. The board was perfect for his need but barely adequate even if he used every inch. There was no way he could cut around the blemish. She could still see him turning the board this way and that, peering to make sure the stain hadn't seeped through to the right side while she'd stood wailing, "I only bled a little!" It wasn't the sort of episode one would be apt to forget.

And this must be why time, tribulation, and Annie's rotten housekeeping hadn't dulled the finish on that exquisite, supposedly precious little table Holly'd been marveling at yesterday. It hadn't been here long enough.

"I wish we could find that wig stand," Cawne was complaining.

What was she to say? "Stick around, my brother's probably making it right now." Holly struggled to keep her voice casual. "I expect Annie will be down in a minute. Come on, let's go holler at her up the stairs."

She wished he'd leave her alone so she could think. If this so-called Mrs. Brown was tricking Roger into supplying duplicates for stolen antiques, Holly must let him know right away so he wouldn't get in any deeper. But was Mrs. Brown the one responsible? Maybe it was Fan who tricked him, or maybe Roger was pulling a fast one on his doting wife. Or maybe they were working the racket together and Holly herself was cast as their innocent accomplice. Who'd ever believe she hadn't come here on purpose to help them rob Cliff House of its valuables?

She was in a more dangerous spot right now than she'd been the instant before that floodlight blew up. And all she could think of to do was act as if she didn't know it.

"Annie," she called, trying to sound normal, "are you almost finished up there? We're trying to find a wig stand."

"A what?" The housekeeper came to the head of the stairs and began picking her way down, cumbered by an armload of soiled bedding. "Just let me get these sheets down to the washtub."

"I'll take them."

"No, dearie. I'm used to it and you're not. She can't help herself, poor soul."

"Oh." Holly stepped back. No wonder Annie never got around to cleaning, if this was the sort of thing she'd been coping with every day by herself. Yet Annie was smiling when she came back to them.

"Now, where did I last see that wig stand? Seems to me we stuck it out in the woodshed behind those boxes of stuff left over from when Mathilde's cousin Lenore's daughter-in-law Delphine closed out her millinery shop."

Sure enough, the precious relic turned up behind a stack of perished cartons filled with bedraggled veiling and artificial flowers. Cawne was aghast.

"Was there no limit to the junk that woman saved? Here's a restoration job for your brother, at any rate," he remarked as he tried to make the broken legs stand upright.

Holly shivered. It would be all too easy for Roger to provide Cliff House with a brand-new genuine antique wig stand. What sort of mess had he gotten his family into?

Chapter 10

"I'd say we've done a creditable day's work, wouldn't you?"

Without waiting for her answer, Geoffrey slung the strap of his camera case over his shoulder. "You won't mind my leaving the rest of the stuff here? It's such a nuisance dragging it back and forth. See you tomorrow."

"Good night," was about all Holly could manage. What jolly sport she was going to have steering him away from the fakes. Geoffrey mightn't know much more about antiques than he did about photography, but he'd surely smell a rat if too many pieces kept turning up in a perfectly preserved state. If only she'd paid more attention to Fan's scrapbook, so she'd know what to stay clear of!

Why did Fan keep such a damning record, anyway? Surely its very existence must prove she at least was innocent. Roger, too, because he knew all about the scrapbook.

No, that didn't follow. Judging from the way she went around ripping other people's property apart in broad daylight, Fan must think she could bulldoze her way through life, doing whatever she pleased and never getting caught. As for Roger, he was fanatical enough about his work to want its records preserved no matter how risky they might be.

One thing sure, Holly had better stop trying to clean up Cliff House. That film of dust over everything here might be all that stood between her and the county jail. What she ought to do was walk straight out this door and keep going.

And how far would she get, half crippled and almost broke? What would she live on? How would she manage without her luggage? And how soon would she be extradited back to Jugtown as an accessory to grand larceny? As it was, she'd have a lovely time trying to convince a jury she'd come here just to get away from Howe Hill. Running away would amount to a confession of guilt.

Holly slumped back to the kitchen and dropped into a battered chair that smelt of Bert Walker. She was wondering whether the relief of warming her sore feet would be worth the effort of opening the oven door when Annie bustled into the room.

"Land alive, dearie, you look like the skin of a nightmare dragged over a gatepost. Doesn't that Professor Cawne know enough not to work a person half to death when she's just out of the hospital? Lean back and rest yourself. I'll pour you a nice cup of tea."

She filled two time-crazed ironstone mugs, topped them up with milk, and passed one to Holly. "There you go, dearie. That's the stuff to put hair on your chest."

"I shouldn't wonder if it did." Annie's tea was a potent brew. Nevertheless, the hot drink did make Holly feel a little better.

Annie dragged another chair close to the stove, fetched her own mug, and settled herself cozily. "There now. It's a Godsend having you for company, dearie. You can't imagine how dismal it's been these past few years with never a soul to talk to but Bert Walker for a little while in the evenings and Earl Stoodley when he takes a mind to poke his nose in, not that Earl's any treat. Anyway, a woman needs another woman. More tea?"

"No thanks, that was fine."

Holly had to smile back at the dumpy old woman in the worn-out housedress. Annie was in this mess as deep as she. Naturally people would think she'd been taking bribes to overlook what was happening, for all her wild talk about footsteps in the night and doors that wouldn't open. How could you run out on somebody so decent and loving, who thought you were a Godsend? Holly gave Annie's wrinkled hand a pat, hauled herself out of the chair by brute force, and went to soak away some of her anxiety in that marvelous zinc bathtub.

Bert was in the rocking chair when she got back downstairs. "Sam dropped me off," he explained. "Said he'd be back about ha'past seven to pick me up. He's gettin' awful considerate all of a sudden."

"Nice for you." Trying to ignore his trollish leer, Holly went to inspect the larder. Tired as she was, she'd rather cook than face another of Annie's suppers.

With supplies so limited, she couldn't vary the menu to any extent, but Bert and Annie probably weren't much for gourmet cooking anyway. She made gravy from bouillon cubes, threw in whatever she could find by way of seasoning, and heated slices of weary leftover beef in the savory sauce. She got a crispy brown crust on the fried potatoes and opened a tin of stewed tomatoes as an antidote to this surfeit of carbohydrates. She thought of hot biscuits but couldn't bear the thought of baking them in such close proximity to Bert's reeking socks. Canned plums and the tag-end of Annie's molasses cake would have to do for dessert.

While things were cooking, Holly nipped outside and picked a few scrawny chrysanthemums from what must once have been a perennial border. Cliff House ought to have formal Victorian flower beds with gorgeous clashes of red and yellow blooms. There should be boxwood and yews clipped into fantastical shapes like chessmen and sitting ducks.

Why couldn't she have thought of aardvarks or zebras or anything but ducks? Now that telltale bloodstain was back in her mind. Now she, like Annie, had a specter to haunt her. What a shame she didn't dare explain to the housekeeper, "That's no ghost you hear. It's just crooks sneaking the Parlett heirlooms out of the house and bringing in copies." If Annie knew that, she'd be laying for them with the dust mop!

Returning to the kitchen with her skimpy bouquet, Holly

caught Annie sidling toward the whiskey bottle, empty glass in hand.

"I thought I might just get myself another little sip, dearie. These raw nights do get into a body's old bones."

Maybe that was why the thieves were so cocky about coming here. Annie did like her nip before supper, and gossip might have spread that Mrs. Parlett's housekeeper reeled to bed dead drunk every night. Fan might have heard some such tale during those early visits to the Women's Circle, and it would be like Fan to act without bothering to find out the tale wasn't true.

Self-sacrificing types like Fan were dangerous. They'd justify anything by insisting they were doing it for unselfish reasons. It struck Holly that her brother might be afraid of his wife, and that he might have reason to be. Though she ought to have been hungry after her strenuous day and unpalatable lunch, she sat down with little appetite.

"My stars, this is a real company meal." Annie unrolled her napkin with a giggle of pure delight. "Flowers on the table and everything. I declare, Bert, I never did see anything to beat this little girl of ours."

The handyman speared a slice of bread with his fork and swabbed it around in the gravy on the platter. "Cripes, I ain't et like this since I was cookee to Lem Halleck at a loggin' camp on the Mirimachi. Mean old brute to work for, but hand 'im a skillet an' a rind o' moldy bacon an' he could turn out a feast fit for the gods."

He was off on one of his yarns, talking and chewing at the same time with equal gusto. Annie nibbled and nodded and sipped her tea like a real lady of the manor. They were having such a lovely time that Holly could feel her own spirits lifting. With a decent meal under her belt, things didn't look so black. By the time Annie and Bert had settled for their postprandial naps and Sam Neill came tapping at the windowpane, Holly was able to go out to him with a halfway cheerful greeting.

"Hi. If you're looking for your uncle, you'll have to wait a while. He and Annie are having their bye-byes."

Neill grinned. "Sleeping it off, eh? They do take their tea pretty strong, I understand."

"Who told you Annie drinks?" Holly snapped out the question so fiercely that Sam gaped at her.

"Bert, I suppose," he replied. "Why?"

"I just hate having people think she's a lush. She isn't."

"If you say so."

Neill turned and began scrambling down the steep hillside, taking it for granted Holly was coming, too. She thought she wouldn't, then she did. Soon, though, she had to call a halt.

"Are we supposed to be taking a quiet stroll?"

The woodcarver paused, his red hair throwing out glints from the lowering sun. "What's the matter? Am I going too fast for you?"

"I have this bad cut on my leg."

"Holly, I'm sorry." He came back to give her a helping hand. "I keep forgetting you'd been hurt. Why didn't you remind me sooner?"

"I should have thought my face would be reminder enough."

Her answer appeared to puzzle Sam Neill for a moment. "Oh," he said at last. "You mean those scars on your cheeks? When I look at you, I don't see them."

If this was a line, it was a beauty. Holly almost started to cry.

"Sam, you can't mean that."

"I suppose what I meant was that I never pay much attention to surface blemishes. You know how it is when you get your hands on a likely hunk of wood. No, I don't suppose you do. Anyway, you don't bother about a few scratches on the bark. You're wondering what's inside."

Holly swallowed hard. "Thanks, Sam. That's what I've been ·hoping somebody would say ever since they took the bandages off. The only other person who claimed he didn't notice was Geoffrey Cawne, but that's because he's too nearsighted."

"That so? What else has he been telling you?" Neill took her arm with a funny, possessive gesture. "I think it'll be easier on your leg if we go on down to the ledge rather than try scrambling back up the hill. The tide's on its way out so we'll be safe enough for a while."

"If you say so. I didn't know there was a ledge."

"You can't see it unless you go to the edge of the cliff and look over, which I don't recommend. It's about a twenty-foot drop most of the way, but there is one path that's not too tough, or didn't use to be. I haven't used it since I was a kid."

He was going slowly, supporting her as best he could, picking steps she could take without too much strain. "The rock broadens out almost like a natural road all the way around the point, and slopes up to make a ramp of sorts at each end. You can drive a car along it if you don't care what happens to your springs. The ledge is flattish and firm to walk on, and if you can't go the distance, we'll find you a soft rock to rest yourself on while I bring the wagon down to get you."

"I'll be all right if we just take it easy. I have to be careful not to take too long a step, that's all."

"We'll watch it."

Sam Neill didn't say any more. Holly was glad enough to be quiet. In the hospital ward she'd never got a moment's peace that wasn't bought with Seconal. At Howe Hill Fan had chattered nonstop. Out here Annie Blodgett was almost as vocal though easier on the nerves.

Geoffrey Cawne was another sociable type. All day long he'd kept up a running commentary. At first she'd been amused, but after that terrible discovery of the stain in the Bible box she'd found his banter hard to take. Her brother was the sole person Holly'd been with for weeks who didn't want to chat, but being with Roger was total noncommunication.

This was a different kind of not talking. It was good to be here with blue serenity above, blue turbulence below, and somebody watching her step for her. She didn't speak again until she felt like it.

"Bay of Fundy. That means *Baie des Fonds,* Bay of Deeps, doesn't it?"

"Some say so," Sam replied. "The early explorers called it *La Baie Française.* In case you didn't know, the Sieur de Monts charted this coast back in 1604. That was before your famous Pilgrim Fathers even started wondering where to buy their seasickness pills."

"They weren't my Pilgrim Fathers. At least I don't think they were. My parents never had time to talk about their ancestors with Roger and me." Or anything else of any importance. "Oh look! There goes a lobsterman out to set his traps."

Sam laughed. "Guess again. That's Ellis Parlett. Can't you see what he's got in his dory?"

"It's so far away." Holly squinted, trying to focus her eyes on the dark oblong that was dragging down the bow of the open rowboat. "All it reminds me of is the chest of drawers in Annie's bedroom."

"Got it first try. Mahogany veneer, circa 1880. Duck behind this rock and make believe we're part of the landscape. If Ellis spots us he'll pretend he's just out for a row."

"But why? What's he up to?"

"Watch," Sam repeated.

The gangly youth in the boat shipped his oars, picked his way forward, and bent over the dresser. As her eyes adjusted to the distance, Holly could see he had with him a length of rope. Something was tied to the end. It looked like a plastic bleach-water jug, and probably was. Lots of lobstermen used them for buoys. Why was Ellis making such a mystery over nothing?

Chapter 11

Slowly and carefully, Ellis Parlett eased the chest of drawers over the dory's gunwale, using one of his oar handles as a lever. It sank with hardly a ripple, leaving the white jug bobbing on the surface. Then he clambered back to the rowing thwart and headed for shore.

"Why did he do that?" Holly whispered. "Why didn't the dresser float? And if he wanted to get rid of it, why did he mark the spot where it sank?"

"First," said Sam, "the dresser didn't float because he filled the drawers with rocks. Second, he's not getting rid of it. He's going to soak it till the veneer peels off. Then he'll haul it up, take it home, and drill some nice, artistic wormholes in the pine boards the veneer was stuck to, give it a few belts with a bicycle chain to antique it some more, sand it down, give it a coat of wax, and then some lucky tourist is going to pick up a nice old pine dresser at a big, fat bargain."

"Sam, you're kidding! Does Claudine know what Ellis is up to?"

Holly was watching Sam's face carefully when she mentioned Claudine, but he only looked amused.

"That kind of amateurish faking couldn't fool anybody who doesn't want to be fooled. You can tell Victorian furniture was machine-made if you take the time to examine it properly. Even if he cuts it down, the proportions will be different from an early piece. I don't condone fraud, but the plain fact is that anybody who buys one of Ellis's fakes may be getting a more solid piece of furniture than if he'd bought the genuine article.

It's all horsefeathers about every colonial farmer's being a master craftsman, you know. Most of the stuff they knocked together was so crude it fell apart pretty fast. That's why there's not all that much of it left. Personally, I'd take Victorian any day."

"So would I," Holly agreed. "I love the stuff. I thought it was just because I'm a clod. By the way," she might as well take the bull by the horns, "what about my brother's work? Do you think there's any possible chance somebody might sometime try to pass off one of his pieces as a genuine antique?"

"Since you ask, I'd say there's every chance in the world," Neill told her frankly.

"But would it work? Is Roger good enough to fool an expert?"

"I'd say he's absolutely first class. As to fooling an expert, I just don't know. To begin with, a person might wonder if he started running across a lot of duplicates. The furniture Roger copies is apt to be one of a kind. It would be unusual for a cabinetmaker to fashion two pieces identically alike, unless they were meant to be used as a pair. Then there's the finish, a certain patina that comes with age. Aside from any distressing —accidental chips, dents, and scratches—you'd normally find a certain amount of crazing or cracking on a varnished or lacquered piece. There'd be some dulling of the surface no matter how well the piece was preserved. I suppose a spectroscopic analysis could be done, if you wanted to get that picky."

"But how many collectors take their spectroscopes to the antique shop? If you use old wood—" Holly stopped abruptly, and Sam knew why.

"That would help to make his work more convincing. Also, Roger doesn't deliberately fake up his finishes, but he does use the original formulae. That could make analysis tricky, especially after some time had elapsed. As to aging a piece enough to fool the average buyer—"

"Whack it with a bicycle chain and stick it under the downspout. I get it. I'm surprised you were willing to involve yourself with such a shady enterprise."

"You've got a tongue on you, young woman. I'm not accusing your brother of anything. You asked me a question and I answered it."

"I know. It's just that—Roger and Fan are such fools!"

That wasn't what she'd meant to say, and Neill knew it.

"Let's say they're so busy doing their thing that they've never taken time to think of the possible consequences."

"It wouldn't matter if they did. Roger would take it as a matter of course if somebody mistook him for Samuel McIntire, and Fan would start wondering how to get a cut of the profits. You must think I'm rotten, talking this way."

"No, Holly, I think you're worried. Why? Has something happened?"

What could she say? "Watching Ellis out there started me wondering, that's all. I suppose I'm disenchanted, if that doesn't sound too arty. This Howe Hill idea seemed so clean and free and innocent when I heard about it back in New York. Then I arrive to find Roger the same cold fish he always was and Fan out vandalizing the neighborhood to give her baby what he wants and—and—people pulling dirty tricks and —oh, I don't want it!"

"I'm sorry."

"Thanks, Sam. Maybe I'm just depressed because I'm not healing fast enough. Maybe it's from being out here in that filthy old house with Mrs. Parlett dying and the vultures circling around her. One vulture, anyway. Would you believe Earl Stoodley practically told me in so many words not to bother doing anything that might help to keep her alive? He's positively slavering to get his pudgy paws on Cliff House."

"Stoodley's enough to depress anybody," Sam agreed. "His trouble is that he'd like to be a bigger frog than this little puddle can hold."

"Then why doesn't he take a running jump for himself and go find a bigger puddle?"

"He knows he hasn't got what it takes to make it anywhere else. Earl's smarter than he looks."

"He'd almost have to be, wouldn't he?"

Sam Neill smiled but did not reply. He was half-lifting her down the last tricky bit to the ledge. When Holly stood on firm ground again, she felt awed. Here, only a few hundred yards from Cliff House, she was in a landscape from Mars.

"What kind of rock is this?" she breathed, afraid to talk loudly lest her voice bring echoes in an unknown tongue. "I've never seen any so—so red."

"That's mud," Sam told her. "The tide comes in with such force that it scrapes up tons of red mud off the bottom of the bay. Everything in its way gets dyed this weird color. Up toward Moncton, even the water looks red. Gives you a strange feeling, looking out over red waves."

"I can imagine," said Holly. "I feel strange right now."

"Are you okay? I hope I haven't worn you out."

"No, I'm fine. It's just this place. It's so overwhelming."

"I suppose it is. I'm used to it, myself. See those caves up under the cliff? I used to come up here with Bert when I was a kid, and explore them while he was doing chores. Mrs. Parlett would have fits. She was always scared to death of the tides. She'd tie a doughnut on a string and dangle it over the edge to lure me back up to the terrace."

"That's cute. I suppose Claudine came, too."

"What makes you think that? Claudine wouldn't be caught dead at Parlett's Point. See what I mean about the ledge?"

Holly was more interested in why Claudine wouldn't come to Parlett's Point and why Sam was so quick to get off the subject, but she had to admit the ledge was a remarkable phenomenon. Fundy's tide had leveled off an almost perfectly flat shelf, just as Sam had told her, with rough slopes at the end where a daredevil driver might just be able to jockey down a car or truck.

And somebody had. Right at her feet was a splotch of crankcase oil. "Look, Sam, somebody's been here since the last high tide."

"Not necessarily. Crankcase oil is pretty sticky and heavy. That stain could have been here for a while. I suppose it must have been some of the kids from the village, though they don't usually risk their old gas-guzzlers on the ledge. The going's slow and it's dangerous to be here at the wrong time. When that tide starts moving, it comes mighty fast. Watch your step here, it looks as though there's been a small rock slide off the edge up above. I wonder how that happened?"

"Rain could have loosened the soil."

"We haven't had rain for upward of two weeks. Now, that's peculiar. Watch out, don't step in it."

Holly moved her foot away from the black puddle. "It's just another glob of oil. We've been seeing dribbles for the past twenty feet or more."

"Right, we've seen dribbles and now a big glob. What do you make of that?"

"Somebody's car needs fixing. Oh, I see what you mean. To have dropped so much oil in one spot, the car must have sat here awhile. Maybe it was because the rocks were falling and the driver didn't want to get hit."

"Then why did he park right under the fall? See how the rocks are lying right in and around the stain? Here's one with a clean underside and oil all over the top."

"Sam, that is odd. It looks as if the rock got dripped on while the car was sitting here. Almost as if the driver might have got out and climbed the cliff himself, and made the rocks fall down."

"This is a strange place to pick," Sam objected. "Also, I don't see why he didn't take the trouble to kick the rocks out of the way before he drove on, rather than risk a skid driving over them."

"Maybe he didn't know they were there. Maybe he couldn't see them because it was dark."

"Come on, Holly! Who'd be fool enough to drive down here at night and try a climb like that?"

Holly caught her breath. Fan and Roger are such fools. She'd said that herself only minutes ago. And Fan's decrepit truck did leak oil terribly. And a rock slide could easily be started by lowering a heavy piece of furniture over the cliff to a truck waiting below. And she hoped to goodness Sam Neill wasn't thinking what she was thinking.

Chapter 12

After that, Holly hardly said a word. Sam must have thought she was exhausted. He took her arm again and, without forcing the pace, kept moving her steadily along. This ledge could become a death trap for anybody who failed to realize the incredible speed and height of Fundy's incoming tide.

So this was why Annie didn't hear those eerie footsteps every night. The thieves couldn't operate unless the tide was right. Even so, what an appalling risk to take! What if the truck stalled, as Fan's had done two mornings ago in front of the library? Holly must have turned white because Sam clamped an arm around her waist and lifted her bodily up the last steep pitch to the road.

"You stay here and rest. I'll bring the wagon around."

"I'm all right," Holly insisted. "I'm just sorry I have to be such a slowpoke. You go on ahead if you're anxious about getting Bert home."

"Don't fret yourself about that old coot. He's either still asleep or bending Annie's ear about what a superman he was fifty years ago. I'm in no hurry, if you're sure you feel up to walking the rest of the way. I suppose it feels good to be out in the air after being cooped up in that place all day."

"You don't know the half of it. It's so gloomy I get these wild urges to sling a few buckets of yellow paint around. Wouldn't Earl Stoodley have a fit?"

He chuckled. "You seem to have Stoodley on the brain."

"That's because I have him underfoot so much. He was here all morning, pestering Geoffrey Cawne."

"Oh, the great professor showed up, did he? I trust he got lots of lovely pictures for his profound and erudite book."

Sam's imitation of Geoffrey was too funny not to laugh at, but Holly was annoyed with herself for doing it. "I hope so. We worked hard enough."

"Who's we?"

"I told you Geoffrey'd asked me to help. I know a lot more about photography than he does."

"That I can believe."

"You don't like him much, do you?"

"I hardly know the guy." Sam took a few more steps, then asked, "How long did he stay?"

"Who?" Holly teased. "Earl or the professor?"

"Both of them."

"Till about one o'clock, then they went to eat. Annie wouldn't feed them."

"Good for Annie. I wouldn't, either."

"Sweet kid, aren't you? Anyway, Geoffrey came back an hour or so later, but your friend Stoodley didn't. He'd found out photography isn't all fun and games, I expect."

Neill stopped in his tracks and stared. "Are you telling me Earl Stoodley let this guy Cawne roam around Cliff House all afternoon without a bodyguard?"

"I think I was supposed to be the bodyguard."

"Oh yeah? What was he taking pictures of?"

"Various objects of historical interest," she replied primly.

"Such as what? Annie in her bathing suit?"

"That remark was neither amusing nor in good taste."

"Then what are you grinning for? Come on, tell me."

"I'm surprised you bother to ask," Holly stalled, wondering what would be safe to mention. The wig stand would do. Roger hadn't made one of those, as far as she could recollect.

"The last was a wig stand brought over from England back before the Revolution. We had to dig it out from behind a pile of old hat trimmings and horsefeed bills dated around 1906.

Earl claims he's inventoried every single item in Cliff House, but I honestly don't see how anybody ever could."

Sam grunted. "Earl talks a good fight. He probably listed the big pieces and lumped the rest under miscellaneous."

"That would be some miscellaneous! The Parletts were always packrats, I gather, and Annie says after old Jonathan died, his wife insisted on saving every last thing that belonged to him. Poor Mrs. Parlett. I wonder if she has any inkling of what's happening. It's so rude of that man, coming up here and pawing through her things while she's lying there helpless. Wouldn't you hate it yourself?"

"I doubt if I'd have much to paw through. I'm a chucker, not a saver. Anyway, I understand Mrs. Parlett's beyond caring now."

"Maybe yes and maybe no. Mrs. Parlett hasn't been seen by a doctor in years. I've been prodding Annie to get him out here, but she won't without Claudine's permission, and Claudine just moans, 'What's the use? He couldn't do anything.' I wish you'd remind her there's been a lot of research done in geriatrics recently."

"What makes you think Claudine gives a hoot?"

"But of course she does. I can tell. She cares terribly."

"Why should she? Mrs. Parlett never gave her the time of day."

"Is that what Claudine tells you?"

"Claudine doesn't tell me anything. It's none of my business. What's eating you, anyway?"

"I'm just trying to understand what's going on. Here's Mrs. Parlett lying helpless, and there's Claudine tearing herself to pieces about it but refusing to call the doctor and refusing to come herself. And here's me smack in the middle, and the more I see of this situation, the less I like it."

"I think you're exaggerating Claudine's concern."

"Sam, I'm not. Bert can bear me out. Look, here he comes now. I'll bet he's looking for us."

He was. "Where the hell have you two been?" he was roaring. "Annie's havin' kitten fits for fear you've eloped an' stuck 'er with the supper dishes."

Holly flushed, but Sam laughed.

"We've been watching Ellis Parlett set a lobster trap," he told his uncle.

"Ayuh? What's he catchin' this time?"

The question was plainly rhetorical. Bert hustled his nephew into the station wagon without waiting for an answer.

"'Night, Holly," Sam called out as he started the motor. "I've got to get this old sculpin home to the television before the dancing girls come on. Hope I didn't wear you out."

"Not a bit," she called back. "I'm anxious to see what Ellis hauls up. Hi, Annie, I'm coming."

She waved the men off, then went in to do the dishes. By the time she'd hung up the tea towels, it was pitch black outside. Holly would have been glad to go to bed, but Annie was all set for another cozy chat.

At least with Annie, a person didn't have to talk back. Holly sat letting the stream of chatter flow over her, nodding her head now and then, not even trying to keep track of what Annie was saying. She had other things to think about. If only the old housekeeper would talk herself out and go to bed! Then Holly could get on with her last chore of the day, the one she most passionately didn't want to perform. At last she'd had all she could take.

"Annie, is there a flashlight I can use?"

"What?" Jerked out of the long-ago, Annie had to pull her thoughts together. "Why yes, dearie. I keep one beside my bed, and there's another in the culch drawer."

"What's a culch drawer?"

Annie couldn't believe Holly had never heard the word before. "It's where you put the culch, of course. Stuff you don't want to throw out but can't think what else to do with."

"You mean you have a special drawer for junk? In this house?" That was the best laugh Holly'd had since she came to Jugtown.

A bit huffily, Annie went to the drawer and fished out the flashlight. "There you are, dearie. I should have thought to give you this sooner. You never know when the power may go off, and I'm not one for oil lamps or candles. If this house ever once got started, it would go up like a bonfire and us with it. I don't know but what I'm more scared of fire than I am of—"

She buttoned her lips and unfastened her apron strings. "Mustn't go wishing trouble on yourself, that's what my mother always said. Well, dearie, let's get to bed. The professor will be here tomorrow to take more pictures, I expect. Isn't he the sweetest man? So famous and distinguished and all, but he acts as natural as us common folks."

Annie patted Holly's hand apologetically. "I don't mean you're common, dearie. Bert says you've even had your picture in the Sears Roebuck catalog. But here you are washing dishes for a living just like me. Not that I ever did it for the pay and not that Aunt Maude ever gave me any, except maybe a little something for Christmas or my birthday, but what did I ever need money for? I had a good roof over my head and three square meals a day and no place to spend it if I'd had it. Count your blessings is what I always tell myself. Would you like a cup of tea before we turn in?"

"No, thanks."

As soon as she'd said no, Holly wished she hadn't. She should have agreed to the tea and contrived somehow to slip a couple of aspirin into Annie's cup, to make the old woman sleep more soundly. Now she'd just have to listen for snores and take her chances.

She waited an eternity before Annie quit puttering back and forth to Mrs. Parlett's room, to the bathroom, to Mrs. Parlett's again, back to the bathroom because she'd heard a faucet dripping, back a third time because Annie was, after all, an old woman. Listening in her own room, Holly dropped into a doze and didn't wake until long after midnight.

By now Annie ought to be safely bedded down if she was

ever going to be. Holly put on her fleece-lined slippers, took the flashlight, and slipped out of her room.

Even in a heavy robe she felt cold as she crept downstairs and through the welter of obstacles in the front hall. She almost fell over the little galleried table. When she realized what it was, she picked it up and carried it with her into the back parlor, where she'd left the Bible box that afternoon.

It took courage to shut herself into that stuffy, overcrowded room. What if there should be such things as ghosts, after all? How would the family specters feel about having a stranger barge in on their nighttime prowls? Holly shoved her thumb down hard on the flashlight button.

Turning on the light made this expedition seem theatrical and silly. She'd been getting herself worked up over nothing. She opened the lid of the Bible box. No, she hadn't.

The ducklike stain showed a slight reddish-brown cast. Four tiny holes arranged in a perfect rectangle marked where Roger had attached his nameplate to hide the stain. Her brother always made a big deal of screwing on those four-inch strips of engraved brass, as though they were some kind of monument to Roger Howe's genius instead of bits of nonsense anybody could remove in about two minutes.

Maybe he had only one nameplate. Maybe he kept screwing it on each finished piece for the benefit of whoever happened to be watching and taking it off again when nobody was around. Charming thought. Holly tilted up the galleried table and peered underneath. By raking the flashlight beam at a sharp angle she could see them: four miniature dents, visible only because she'd known what to look for; but definitely, sickeningly, damningly there.

Chapter 13

In sudden panic, Holly snapped off the flashlight. Why hadn't she drawn the blinds? Out on this lonely spit of land, anybody might come prowling.

"I've got to get back upstairs."

She was talking aloud. The horrible part was that her words evoked a strange, rustling echo as though her mind were answering back. Blundering through the clutter, she groped for the door and grasped the knob like a lifeline. It turned, but the door wouldn't open.

"I've locked myself in."

For a second she was more annoyed than scared. She'd done silly things like this back in New York. All she had to do was switch on the overhead light and find something to force the catch with. Then she remembered. Old-fashioned locks didn't snap shut by themselves. They worked by keys, and keys needed hands to turn them. And there was no key on her side of the door.

"Take it easy, Holly. You're safe enough. Nothing's going to get at you. Don't scream for Annie. Either she's locked in, too, or else she might come downstairs and get hurt. Stay cool and keep your mouth shut. Quit rattling the knob. Quit shoving at the panels. Go over to the sofa and sit down."

Holly tried to listen to her own good advice. If this was what had been happening to Annie, she was in no danger. Sooner or later the door would be unlocked and she could get out. That didn't make it any easier to be penned up like this, not knowing who or what was her jailer.

Why not open a window and jump out? Into what? Even though she knew this was a risky thing to do, Holly crept toward the nearest oblong of darkened glass.

It was black as pitch outside. The clouds that had started rolling in while she and Sam Neill were down on the ledge now blotted out every star. There was just one lone dot of phosphorescence out in the bay.

That dot was a puzzler. It moved gently up and down, but never drifted from its position. It couldn't be a boat's riding light; it didn't shine but simply glowed, like the luminous dial on a clock. Holly was grateful for the dot, it helped take her mind off being trapped. What on earth could it be?

Then she picked out the shape of a small boat sliding out from under the bluff, and she knew. That mysterious glow had to be Ellis Parlett's plastic jug, daubed with luminous paint, so he could find it in the dark. Ellis must be going back to collect his new antique.

But why? The dresser had only been in the water a few hours. Surely the veneer wouldn't even have begun to peel. Was that really Ellis, or was somebody about to rob his trap?

Holly wished she knew more about boats. She thought she remembered Ellis's had been pointed at both ends. This one had a lump on its stern that she finally decided must be an outboard motor cocked up out of the water. As her eyes grew more accustomed to the dark, she made out long sticks moving up and down in steady rhythm. Why row against the ferocious currents around Parlett's Point if you had a motor to do the job for you?

Maybe the motor was out of gas. Then why not go and get some? Because motors made noise. But who would hear? Only herself, Annie, and possibly Mathilde Parlett. What could they do about a motorboat out in the bay?

They could tell people it had been there. If Annie heard an outboard off Parlett's Point at this ungodly hour, she'd be sure to mention that fact to Bert Walker, then Bert would spread the joke about somebody trying to rob Ellis Parlett's so-called lobster trap.

According to Sam, everybody in town knew about Ellis's Tom-Sawyerish skulduggery, or ought to; but how many would know Ellis had been out there this particular evening? Sam did, of course. Could that be Sam in the boat?

Why should it be? He'd kidded with his uncle about watching Ellis, she'd heard him. Bert could have passed on the joke to a few of his cronies downtown before settling down to watch the dancing girls. Surely that wasn't the old man himself out there? Holly got the impression of a much burlier figure, though that could be because he was wearing oilskins or more likely a life jacket. It would be crazy to be out there without one on a night like this.

Anyway, the boat was definitely going to the buoy. Its glow was hidden now by the low hull. The boatman was crouching over the side. Hauling on the line to raise the dresser, she'd bet. Yes, there was something big and black breaking water. He'd take the rocks out, surely, before he got it into the boat. No, he was doing something else, she couldn't imagine what.

The boat rocked, the dresser disappeared. The luminous dot was dipping and rising on the roiled water, the oars were churning toward shore. The boatman hadn't found the chest worth keeping, but why had he expected to? Who'd leave something of value bobbing around on a rope tied to a bleach bottle?

The explanation was perfectly simple. She was asleep and having a nightmare. None of this was real, she wasn't locked in. She tried the door again and it opened. Then she whacked her knee against the jamb. The pain was no illusion.

All right, she'd been locked in and let out. Was she going back to bed and risk meeting whoever had been playing games with the key, or wasn't she?

The heck with it. She'd already been brave enough for one night. Holly shut the door again, dragged a heavy armchair against it, and went back to the sofa, to shiver miserably until the black windowpanes turned to gray and Cliff House felt less like a house of horrors.

Chapter 14

When she at last got back to Cousin Edith's bed it seemed like a haven of safety, but Holly was too keyed-up to stay in it long. She was downstairs before eight o'clock. Annie was there, slumped at the kitchen table, sipping at the inevitable cup of tea.

It was colder this morning. The old housekeeper was huddled into a blue worsted cardigan, darned at the elbows, stained down the front. How many hours had she sat there alone, unkempt, woebegone, hanging on and doing her best? As she started to get up, Holly pushed her gently back into her chair.

"Sit still and drink your tea. I'm going to scramble us some eggs. Do you think Mrs. Parlett would eat them?"

"I don't know's I dare give her any, dearie. Gruel and soup's about all I can get down her these days. I'm afraid anything solid might stick in her throat."

"I do wish you'd have the doctor," Holly sighed. "This is too much responsibility for you to handle alone."

"I know, dearie, but what can I do? Claudine won't stand for it. He'd send her to the hospital, then they'd be sticking tubes into her instead of letting her go to her Maker in peace. Claudine doesn't hold with that, and neither do I. When my time comes, dearie, I want you to promise you won't let them keep me alive for no good reason."

What was Holly to say? She'd be long gone by then, she hoped. She settled for a smile and a pat, and went on breaking eggs. They dawdled shamefully over breakfast. If Geoffrey

Cawne intended to shoot more pictures today, he surely wouldn't arrive before nine.

He wasn't coming at all. Holly was nibbling at a last piece of toast she didn't particularly want when the phone rang.

"Holly? Geoff here. Looks as though I shan't be able to make it today. Stoodley has to go up to Moncton."

"Can't you come without him?"

"To be quite frank, I'd rather not risk it. Unless I could get Miss Parlett to chaperone? Do you suppose there's any hope?"

Holly smiled grimly into the phone. "There's no harm in asking."

"I've half a mind to try. If she says yes, may we simply barge along?"

"Barge ahead. We'll be here."

Holly put up the receiver and turned to Annie, who'd been pretending not to eavesdrop. "Earl Stoodley's gone to Moncton and the professor doesn't want to come alone. He's going to see if he can get Claudine."

Annie shook her untidy gray head. "Seems like the smarter they are, the dumber they act. He's lived here long enough to know better. Claudine vowed never to set foot across this threshold and she never will, not if she lives to be two hundred and a day. Nor will Ellis, as long as she's around to stop him."

"But why not? What did Claudine and Mrs. Parlett fight about?"

"Land alive, child, they never fought about anything. Far's I know, they never even passed the time of day."

"But that's crazy! Annie, I can't believe this."

"That's because you don't know the whole story, dearie." Annie folded her hands in her lap and said no more.

"Aren't you going to tell me?" Holly prodded.

"I don't know if I should. It's not a thing for a young lady to hear."

"Annie, I'm no kid. I'm a New York model and whatever your story is, you can bet I've heard worse. Come on, I have a right to know."

"Well, all right. I s'pose you do. It started a long time ago, when I was just a little girl myself. I was still living with my own folks then. Uncle Jonathan and Aunt Maude had been married a fair while, but they didn't have any children. They'd drive out to see us sometimes on a Sunday and Uncle Jonathan would give us young ones those big copper pennies they used to have. I've probably told you this part."

"You have," said Holly. "Go on."

"Yes, dearie. Anyway, as I started to say, they were living here at Cliff House and naturally Aunt Maude had a hired girl to help with the cleaning and all. To make a long story short, this young hussy went and got herself in the family way, and she swore up and down Uncle Jonathan was responsible. Uncle Jonathan said she was lying, and Aunt Maude believed him. My mother said Aunt Maude probably had reason to, seeing as they'd never had any babies of their own, though I suppose I shouldn't repeat that."

She fluttered a bit, then settled back to her story. "Anyway, Aunt Maude stuck by Uncle Jonathan even when this snip of a Myrtle dragged him into court with a trumped-up yarn about him forcing his way into her bedroom and such tales as you'd think they'd have thrown her out for a barefaced liar. But I'll be switched if she didn't get the jury on her side. It was all men in those days, you know, and some said if they hadn't nailed Jonathan Parlett as the father, Myrtle could have turned around and laid it on to any one of them. So they found him guilty and the judge said he'd have to pay the mother fifteen dollars a week support money till the child was sixteen years old, or go to jail. That was a lot of money then."

"But what does that have to do with Claudine?"

"Why, Myrtle's son was Claudine's father. Claude, Myrtle called him. That was what really cooked her goose with Aunt Maude. She'd had a twin brother called Claude, because it rhymed with Maude, I expect. Maude was a popular name in those days. My mother's name was Maude, too. Lillian Maude."

Annie tried to pretend she wasn't rubbing away tears. "Where was I? Oh, about Uncle Claude. He was killed in the Boer War and Aunt Maude never got over losing her twin. If she'd had a boy of her own, she was going to name him after him. But she never did, and then this trollop Myrtle went and stuck his name on to her own brat."

"That was pretty rotten," Holly had to admit.

"Yes, it was about as bad an insult as one woman could give another. Aunt Maude never forgave Myrtle, and I don't know's I would have, either, though I don't think I'd have taken it out on the boy. Claude Jonathan Parlett was what Myrtle told the town clerk to put on his birth certificate, though he'd no more right to the name than a tomcat. That boy was the spitting image of Big Charlie Black, and from all accounts he had reason to be. Charlie was a handsome devil, in his day."

"What happened to him?"

"He left Jugtown right after the trial. Myrtle stuck around collecting her fifteen dollars a week till Claude's sixteenth birthday, then she went off to be with Charlie, leaving Claude here to fend for himself. Folks felt sorry for him and offered him the odd job here and there, but Claude was never one for work. His mother had filled him with too many fairy tales about being born to better things.

"He tried to pester Uncle Jonathan for money, but Aunt Maude put a stop to that. She claimed if Uncle Jonathan gave Claude so much as one cent he wasn't forced to, folks might start thinking he was the real father, after all. I daresay she was right, but it was hard on the boy. I remember Claude coming here to Cliff House one rainy night, huddled up inside an old sweater somebody'd given him. I was living here myself by then. Maude would never have another hired girl, of course. Anyway, I couldn't help feeling sorry for Claude, but Aunt Maude turned him away as if he'd been a case of walking smallpox. She claimed he was just play-acting to work on her sympathies."

"Aunt Maude doesn't sound as if she had many sympathies to work on," Holly couldn't resist saying.

"Oh, she wasn't one to be taken in. Claude got by, one way and another. We went to war with Hitler in 1939 and for want of anything better to do, Claude enlisted. He never got farther overseas than Halifax, but he'd come back here on leave and swagger around in his uniform as if he was General Montgomery. I must admit he cut a dashing figure. Lots of girls in the village would have jumped at the chance to go to the pictures with Claude Parlett. Myself included, if you want the truth. But he never asked me and I wouldn't have dared anyway, on account of Aunt Maude."

Annie wet her throat with a sip of cooling tea. "After the war, Claude went off somewhere and folks sort of forgot about him. Then Aunt Maude died. Claude must have seen the death notice somewhere. The funeral was hardly over when he rolled into town, thinking he'd win Uncle Jonathan over now that the old battle-axe was gone. That's what he always called Aunt Maude."

"How did he make out?" Holly asked.

"He didn't. Uncle Jonathan wasn't around. He'd started going off to Montreal on business trips, or so he said. But one day a year or so after Aunt Maude died, Uncle came back with the sweetest little black-haired lady I ever did see hanging on his arm. 'Annie,' he says to me, 'this is my wife, Mathilde.'

"Well, I was so flustered I didn't know what to say. I just put my arms around the pair of them and started to cry and say I hoped they'd be happy. And I tell you, dearie, they were. Mathilde just brought this old house to life. She was the happiest person I've ever known, though the Lord knows she'd had her share of troubles. Her first husband and their only child had died together of what they used to call infantile paralysis. She'd been left without a penny to live on, so she'd gone to work running a switchboard. That was how Uncle Jonathan got to meet her. It was in some office he used to visit on business. Monkey business I called it, when I found out about Mathilde."

Annie chortled. "Who could blame him? Mathilde told me after he popped the question, she drew every last penny of her savings out of the bank and blew it on a trousseau that would make him proud to be seen with her. Uncle Jonathan thought that was great, her fixing herself up to please her husband. He said she'd never want for anything after that, and she never did.

"He bought her a washing machine and a trip to Paris, and they had parties with friends of theirs coming all the way from Montreal and dancing to the gramophone. That didn't happen too often to suit me, I can tell you. They'd get me in from the kitchen, I'd take off my apron and dance with the rest of 'em.

"Mathilde was nice as pie to me. When they went off somewhere, she'd always leave me a big box of chocolates and some new magazines to read. She even made Uncle Jonathan buy me a nice radio to keep me company. It's been broken now for quite a while. I wish Earl Stoodley would cough up the money to fix it, but I don't suppose he ever will."

Annie sighed, then perked up again. "When Uncle Jonathan went away by himself on trips, Mathilde would take me up to Moncton or down to Saint John. Sometimes we'd stay overnight. We'd eat in restaurants and go to the pictures and into stores, and she'd buy me a dress or a pair of shoes or something —even if I didn't need 'em. Oh, I just loved Mathilde!"

Chapter 15

This time Holly didn't try to break the silence. After a while, Annie dried her tears and went on with her story. "Finally, Uncle Jonathan died. He was well into his eighties by then and we knew it was coming, but Mathilde took it awful hard. She was never the same after he went."

"She must have been pretty old herself by then," said Holly, thinking of that incredibly ancient body in the bed upstairs.

"I never thought of Mathilde as being old."

Annie threatened to lapse into another silent reverie. Holly was getting impatient. "But where does Claude come back into the story?"

"Land's sake, I forgot we were talking about Claude. Where was I?"

"He'd come back and Jonathan was off marrying Mathilde."

"Oh yes. Well, once Claude realized he wasn't going to get anything that way, he tried another tack. I don't know's I ever mentioned it, but Uncle Jonathan had a brother William. It was Jonathan who got Cliff House when their father died, him being the older son, but William had his share of the money fair and square, and ought to have been well-fixed for life."

"But he wasn't?"

Annie shook her head. "William was a lovely man, but he'd no head for money. The Parletts had always been money-makers, and William thought he had to be one, too; though he'd have done better to sit tight and live on what he had. As it was, if some promoter came along with a scheme to pump gold out of sea water or manufacture hand-embroidered buggy whips just when folks were all selling their buggies to buy automobiles, William would be first in line to buy shares in the company. I can remember Uncle Jonathan getting him up here and trying to talk some sense into him, but William wouldn't listen. At last he got so peeved at always being in the wrong that he wouldn't come any more, and wouldn't take a cent from Uncle Jonathan even after he'd run through pretty much all his father had left him.

"William was married to one of the White girls. Abigail, her name was. Aunt Maude never liked Abigail much. She thought William should have picked somebody with more gumption. Abigail was always kind of a dreamy soul, just went along with whatever William wanted to do."

Annie wiped her eyes again and went on with the family saga. "William and Abigail had three children, two boys and a girl. Not having any young ones of his own, Uncle Jonathan naturally thought the world of his niece and nephews. Alice was his pet, being the baby and the only girl. My, how he doted on that child! Then the war came and both the sons were killed at Bastogne. They always seem to stick the Canadians right up in the front lines, no matter what.

"Anyway, that made Alice more precious than ever. And would you believe that devil Claude Parlett started courting her on the sly? He was a lot older than she, but he was handsome and smooth-talking. Next thing we knew, Claude and Alice had run off and got married. Alice was always a little weak in the head, if you want my personal opinion, but she could be stubborn as a mule."

"I'll bet her family had a fit."

"They did that and then some. For once, Jonathan and William were on the same side. They and Abigail and Mathilde all tried to persuade Alice to have the marriage annulled, but she ranted and raved and vowed she'd follow her Claudie to the ends of the earth, married or not, so they had to give in.

"Uncle Jonathan took it worse than Alice's own parents did. He'd had his will all made out leaving everything to her after Mathilde died, but he tore it up and told her point blank he'd deed Cliff House and all that went with it over to the town before he'd let Claude lay one finger on anything of his. So then he was on the outs with William and Abigail again. Much as they despised Claude, they couldn't turn their backs on the only child they had left."

"You can't blame them for that," said Holly. "Where did Claude and Alice go?"

"They didn't go, they stayed. Claude moved into the bedroom that had always been Alice's, and there he roosted. Somehow he'd managed to finagle a little pension out of the army. That and Alice's parents was what they lived on, mostly. William and Abigail didn't last long once they had Claude on their hands. Mathilde claimed they died of broken hearts, and I expect she was right."

"I shouldn't be surprised. What happened after the parents died?"

"Nothing much. Alice had Claudine right away and Ellis ten years later, so that gave them an allotment from the government. Claude tried a little rumrunning, so I'm told, but he drank more than he sold so that fell through. The house got shabbier and the kids ran around looking like two orphans of the storm. Alice wasn't much of a hand at making do. She'd grown up thinking she was going to be an heiress, you see. I think she still had hopes, till Uncle Jonathan died and it turned out he'd done exactly what he'd said he would.

"That was the cap sheaf. Claude took to drinking worse than ever. Then one morning he went out to haul lobster traps, plastered as usual. He caught his foot in a line and went overboard, and that was the end of Claude Parlett. Everybody thought Alice was well rid of him, but she carried on something fierce. She shut herself up and wouldn't let anybody near her. I went myself, for old times' sake, but she wouldn't see me. She claimed I was down on Claude like the rest of them, which was true enough. Next thing I heard, she was sick in bed and Claudine was taking care of her, don't ask me how."

"Wouldn't Mathilde help them?"

"Mathilde wasn't any too well herself by then, dearie. Dr. Walker said it was hardening of the arteries. She'd got it into her head she had to hang on to what there was because it was all she had left of Jonathan. Finally she got so bad she wouldn't even part with enough money to buy groceries. I had to go to court and have her declared incompetent or we'd have starved to death. That's how Earl Stoodley got to be a trustee. He's always got his nose into everything, one way or another. They named Claudine along with him because she was of age by then, and Alice sent word she was too sick to serve."

"How come Claudine agreed?"

"She was none too willing, I can tell you. Claude and Alice had always dinned it into her and Ellis that their father ought to be Uncle Jonathan's rightful heir. After he was drowned, Alice claimed it was the awful way he'd been treated by his so-called father that drove him to it. Ellis was too little to take it in, I expect, but Claudine took every word for gospel. I suppose they had to have some reason to hold their heads up.

"Anyway, when it came to being a trustee, Claudine got up on her high horse and said she'd do her duty but she'd never set foot on the property till her family got what they were morally entitled to. So that's why Professor Cawne isn't going to get Claudine Parlett out here this morning or any other morning."

"And she's still nursing her sick mother?"

"No, she isn't." Annie pushed back her chair and got rheumatically to her feet.

"Why? What happened to Alice?"

"What generally happens? The way I feel this morning, I shouldn't wonder if it happened to me before long. You wouldn't care to give me a hand upstairs, I don't suppose? Mrs. Parlett's mattress hasn't been turned in a dog's age. I thought maybe the two of us could lift her into a chair long enough to redd the place up a little."

"Is she heavy to lift?"

"I don't suppose she weighs eighty pounds. She used to be a fine figure of a woman, but you'd never know it to see her now."

Chapter 16

No, Holly thought a few minutes later, you'd never know it. Mrs. Parlett lay curled up like a dead caterpillar, yellow claws hooking out from the sleeves of a beautiful peach-colored silk nightgown.

"Mathilde had a dozen of those nightgowns," said Annie. "Said she bought 'em to keep Jonathan's mind off other women. Aunt Maude would have bitten out her tongue sooner than say a thing like that."

"I can see why he married Mathilde," Holly replied drily.

"Aunt Maude was a good woman, dearie, but I have to admit Mathilde was a lot more fun to live with. She'd be singing and laughing and running out to pick flowers—now, where did I put those pillow cases?"

"Right there on the night stand. You don't want them yet, do you? I thought we were going to get her up and strip the bed."

"Oh my, yes. I tell you, my head's going. All right, dearie, but we'd better wrap her up well. One good chill could carry her off, not that it wouldn't be a blessing, but still—"

Annie fussed over her patient. She must truly have loved Mathilde, Holly thought, but reason told her there was more to be preserved here than Mrs. Parlett's tenuous hold on life. Cliff House was Annie's home, too. What would become of her when Mrs. Parlett died?

And how could this ancient puppet go on breathing much longer? Holly held her own breath as they lifted the fragile body in its cocoon of velvet comforters and laid it on the brocaded chaise longue. Mathilde must have loved to lie here and watch the clouds flying by outside. Could she see them now? The eyes were half open. They didn't seem to be focusing on anything, but Holly made sure Mathilde's head was turned toward the window, just in case.

She seemed no worse for having been moved. After they'd done the bed, Holly suggested, "Annie, why don't we take Mrs. Parlett into your room and give this one a good airing? It's awfully stuffy."

It was worse than stuffy. Though Annie had done her best, there was a pervading odor of body wastes and general mustiness. Annie thought it over.

"I don't know why we couldn't. There's an old wheel chair in the back bedroom. We could move her in that, easy as pie. I'll get it."

Annie came back pushing a golden oak contraption with huge wire wheels. They squeaked dreadfully on their rusted axles. Holly found some expensive face cream on Mathilde's dresser that had gone rancid in the jar and lathered the joints until the wheels turned smoothly. Then it was no job at all to shift the flaccid body.

While Annie fussed over Mrs. Parlett and made helpful suggestions about a nice cup of tea, Holly vacuumed, dusted, scrubbed, even took the heavy blue velvet draperies out to the clothesline and whacked out clouds of dust with a wire beater. Then she carried them back upstairs and rehung them over windows that had got their first washing in years. By the time they got Mrs. Parlett back into bed, the room was cheery, the air was pure, and the unhealed cut on Holly's thigh was oozing ominously.

"You did too much, dearie," Annie clucked. "You'd better go straight to your own bed."

"I want a bath first."

Holly got cleaned up, found a roll of gauze and some sterile pads, and rebandaged her cut, praying it wasn't going to need more stitches. She should have known better than to do so much. Anyway, Mathilde Parlett should rest more comfortably tonight, whether she knew it or not.

Knowing that if she didn't go down to supper Annie would insist on struggling up to her with a tray, Holly put on her housecoat and limped to the kitchen. Bert was ensconced in his chair by the stove. He leered when he caught sight of the elegant robe.

"'Fraid you got yourself gussied up for nothin' tonight, sis. Sam took his mother down to Saint John. She started havin' pains, so they're goin' to operate soon's they get the knife sharpened."

"Oh, that's too bad. I'm so sorry."

"So's your brother. He's chewin' nails an' spittin' tacks 'cause Sam didn't show up today. That Mrs. Brown's been writin' letters again."

"I'm curious about Mrs. Brown. Have you ever met her, Bert?"

"Not to say met her. I seen her once when she come to the shop. Brassy hair an' paint on 'er face an' dressed like 'er own granddaughter. She had on bright green stockin's over the knobbiest pair o' legs I ever did see. Tough as a boiled owl, like all them New York women."

"I'm a New York woman."

"Aw, you don't count. Wouldn't want to pour out a little snort for a poor old man, would you? I'm all in but the toenails, an' they're rattlin'."

"So am I."

Nevertheless, Holly fixed Bert's drink. She felt a tiny bit better for knowing there actually was a Mrs. Brown, even if she couldn't see how Mrs. Brown might fit into the strange and ugly picture that was developing.

That leg was really giving her a hard time. It was as well Sam wouldn't be coming tonight. She was in no shape for another of his quiet strolls. What would they do when it got too cold to be out? Sit in his wagon, maybe.

No they wouldn't. As soon as his mother got better, Sam Neill would be off on another job somewhere. And where would Holly Howe be?

Chapter 17

By morning, Holly was in bad shape. A hot redness was spreading from the cut toward her groin. If she didn't get an antibiotic soon, they'd need a new hired girl at Cliff House.

She dressed carefully, knowing she wouldn't be able to manage a second trip upstairs. By gritting her teeth and holding tight to the stair rail, she made it down to the kitchen. As usual, Annie was already there.

"Annie," she said, "I've got to see a doctor right away."

"Dearie, what's wrong? Are you in pain? Is it your leg?"

"Yes. How do I reach him? Should I phone for an appointment?"

"Far's I know, you just go to his office and sit there till he calls you in. That's how it always used to be. Bert can drive you down. He'll be along sooner or later to bring the groceries. Claudine usually calls about now to see what I need."

As if on cue, the telephone rang. Holly cried, "I'll get it," but for once Annie was the nimbler of the two. Holly had to listen in agony while Annie prattled on about tea and flour and what a grand job her new helper was doing. At last she literally couldn't stand it any longer, and took the receiver from Annie's hand.

"Claudine, this is Holly Howe. I have to see the doctor as soon as possible. My leg is bothering me badly. I think I can get my sister-in-law to pick me up, but how do I reach—oh, would you? That would be wonderful. No, I understand. I won't. Thank you so much."

She hung up. "Claudine said Dr. Walker has office hours

from nine to twelve on Saturdays. She's going to let him know I'm coming. Now please God Fan can come right away. Oh, and we're not to let Fan inside the house, so get ready to stand guard with the broomstick."

"Cat's foot! A lovely woman like her."

Annie had never laid eyes on Fan, but she was ready to endow her with all the virtues for Holly's sake. Holly wasn't. Fan found her ready and waiting on the front porch when she drove up in answer to Holly's call, about half an hour later.

Holly limped to meet her. "Hi, Fan. Thanks for coming to the rescue."

"You know me, everybody's errand girl." Fan was obviously none too pleased at not getting a peek into Cliff House. "How's it going?"

"Not bad, aside from this blasted leg. Annie's a dear and Mrs. Parlett's no bother. The house is a mess. Now I know what you must have gone through when you first came to Howe Hill."

That turned the trick, as she'd known it would. Fan launched into a tale of her own tribulations that lasted until they got down to the doctor's. Holly'd heard all about it before, but she didn't mind listening again. Fan deserved some reward for being so helpful.

"Thanks, Fan," she said as she eased her sore leg down to the sidewalk. "You're sweet to do this for me."

"What about afterward? Shall I pick you up?"

"I'm supposed to check in with Claudine. She does the shopping for Cliff House on Saturdays and either Bert or Earl Stoodley delivers, so I expect I'll get sent up with the groceries."

Fan scowled. "I was hoping we'd have a chance to visit. I miss you, Holly. Roger's always so absorbed in his work. And as for that new helper, forget it. I might get a good morning out of Neill, but that's about it. You're not missing anything there, believe me. By the way, how's it coming with Geoff Cawne? Has he called you yet?"

"He came up on Thursday and spent the whole day taking photographs. He was coming again yesterday, but Earl Stoodley wasn't around."

"What's Earl Stoodley got to do with his coming?"

"Earl's the bodyguard. There are some real antiques mixed in with the junk. If anything turns up missing when they settle the estate, Geoffrey doesn't want to be accused of having pinched it."

"If the place is in such a mess, how would they know?"

"They'd know. Everything's been inventoried and the lawyers have the list. Earl says they've listed everything from the mice in the pantry to the spiders in the attic."

Let Fan think that over. Holly turned toward the doctor's office.

"Thanks for the ride. I'll phone if Claudine says I can have some time to drop in at Howe Hill. If you don't hear from me, you'll know I've gone back to Cliff House."

"Call me anyway. I want to know what the doctor says."

In a surprising burst of sisterly affection, Fan touched her chapped lips to Holly's scarred cheek before she started the old truck again and clattered off.

Dr. Walker's house was the second neatest on Queen Street. Its shingles were stained a rich tobacco-spit brown, its trim freshly picked out in green enamel. Dr. Walker himself looked like a clean and shaven twin to Bert, and must be a relative. He was no bumpkin; his diploma was from McGill, his manner competent and assured. He wasted no time on small talk, but got Holly up on the examining table, poked and prodded, asked, "Does it hurt when I press here?" and seemed quite pleased when she said it did. He asked what medication she'd been on, jabbed an enormous needleful of something into her thigh, wrote a prescription in a totally illegible hand like a real New York doctor, and indicated Holly's visit was at an end.

She wasn't ready to leave, however. "Dr. Walker," she began, "Claudine may have mentioned I'm working out at Cliff House."

"Don't overdo. Stay off that leg as much as you can."

"Thanks, but what I wanted to ask you was, can't anything be done for Mrs. Parlett?"

"I can't tell you. I haven't seen her for several years."

"I know, that's what worries me. It doesn't seem right. Annie Blodgett's the kindest person imaginable, but she's not a trained nurse and I don't think it's fair for her to have the whole responsibility."

Dr. Walker moved her toward the door. "Miss Howe," he said, "the last time I saw Mrs. Parlett was over five years ago. I gave an opinion then that she'd be dead very soon, perhaps in a matter of days. Immediately after that, I went abroad for a year. When I came back, I was astounded to hear Mrs. Parlett was still alive. I've never been asked to visit her since I got back, and I see no need to. Annie must be handling the case better than I could, trained or not. If that leg hasn't begun to clear up by Wednesday, you'd better come to the office again. Evening hours are seven to nine."

So that was that and here she was, out on the sidewalk with a prescription in her hand and a flea in her ear. Holly walked over to the drugstore and treated herself to coffee and green apple pie at the soda fountain while she waited for the druggist to find his eyeglasses, count out pills into a nice old-fashioned cardboard pillbox the size of a postage stamp, and peck out a label on a typewriter the local antique dealers must be itching to get their hands on.

Now she'd better go report to Claudine. What else was there to do? Holly shoved her pills into the oversized model's handbag she still didn't feel dressed for the street without, and went over to the antique shop.

Chapter 18

Claudine must still be shopping. This had to be Ellis minding the shop. He didn't look a bit like his chic, dark-haired sister, though he was rather attractive in a weedy, Bambi-eyed sort of way. Maybe he was a throwback to Myrtle the naughty housemaid.

He must be at least twenty, but had the softness of youth on him. In spite of fuzzy brown sideburns and jeans amateurishly studded with shiny chrome rivets, Ellis gave the impression that he'd either freeze in terror or leap for the old briar patch if she made a wrong move. Holly closed the door gently and spoke as if she were addressing a wounded sparrow.

"Good morning, I'm Holly Howe. Your sister is expecting me."

Ellis gargled something that could have been, "She said to wait," and made a furtive gesture toward a splat-backed chair. Holly took it gladly and perched her sore leg on a nearby milk can.

"You don't mind, do you? Dr. Walker told me to keep it up."

Her reluctant host didn't seem to care what she did so long as she didn't expect him to get too close. To calm his jumpiness, Holly started explaining about her accident and its consequences. Ellis at last ventured on an anecdote of his own, about one time when he'd been out in the boat and got a fishhook stuck in his hand.

Like most shy people, Ellis was unstoppable once he'd got started. Before long he'd told Holly far more about that fishhook than she cared to know. She gave up listening, just smiled and nodded and let her eyes roam around the shop.

It wasn't hard to pick out samples of Ellis's handiwork now that she knew what to look for. The proportions were wrong, and evidently the manufacturers hadn't always been choosy about the quality of pine that underlay their veneers. Ellis had filled in the cracks and knotholes with a whitish substance that reminded Holly of trodden chewing gum on a wet sidewalk.

There was a kind of terrifying innocence about these faked-up pieces. Maybe Ellis didn't let his conscience realize he was being a swindler, any more than the wreckers of early days thought of themselves as murderers when they lit beacon fires to lure ships on the reefs so they could plunder the cargoes. They'd been concentrating on their own need to survive.

And what about herself? How often had she posed for advertisements with atmosphere-polluting aerosol bombs or plastic gadgets that would serve no useful purpose and clutter up the planet forevermore; and thought only of how glad she was to get the work? At least she wouldn't be exposed to that sort of temptation any more. There was something to be said for being hideous.

But she wasn't hideous. From where she sat, Holly could catch her reflection in a walnut-framed mirror. The scars on her cheeks had faded to straight lines. The pucker at the corner of her left eye was hardly noticeable. She could even pretend it added a whimsical quirk to her glance. The air up here was giving her complexion more color and sparkle than she'd been able to get with cosmetics in New York.

Her hair, now that it wasn't constantly getting bleached or streaked or dyed to suit some art director's whim, was settling down to a pleasant tawny brown that exactly matched the silk scarf she'd tied high around her neck to hide the gouge under her left ear. She was feeling a little better about herself when Geoffrey Cawne strolled in off the street.

It must have taken him all this time to work up nerve enough to tackle Claudine. They'd barely exchanged hello's when the trustee herself came into the shop, pushing a wire shopping cart. Holly's newly boosted ego took a sudden dip. Why hadn't she noticed before that Claudine Parlett was an absolute knockout?

Maybe it was because today those frozen features had thawed. Claudine's cheeks were flushed, her gray-brown eyes alight, her lips voluptuous, coral-tinted curves. The few silver highlights in her straight black hair could have been put there deliberately for a touch of sophisticated chic.

She'd played up the gray cleverly with silver jewelry set in turquoise. There were flecks of turquoise in her heather-gray skirt and jersey. She'd have turned heads on Fifth Avenue. If Sam Neill wasn't romancing Claudine Parlett, then much as Holly hated to admit it, he was missing something pretty special.

Whether her physical attractions had any effect on Geoffrey Cawne, Holly couldn't tell. His certainly weren't having any on her. He explained, he cajoled, he turned on his smile, then turned it off again. He almost, but not quite, began to yell. He might as well have argued with a gatepost.

All Claudine would reply was, "I'm sorry, Professor, but I said I wouldn't and I won't. If Earl Stoodley hasn't time to go with you, you'll simply have to wait till Cliff House is open to the public."

"But that might be years from now!"

"I hope so."

There was passion behind those three short words. Claudine did care about keeping alive that old woman she wouldn't go to see, no matter what anybody said. Why?

Looking at Claudine's superb grooming, her attractively arranged shop, Holly thought Claudine must always have been drawn to beauty. According to Annie, there'd been little enough of it in her young life. What if, wandering alone, the neglected child had met Mathilde in her lovely Paris clothes, singing and dancing among the flowers? What if the vivacious Frenchwoman, perhaps bored with isolation and yearning after her own dead child, had befriended Jonathan's great-niece on the sly? With so little else to pin her dreams on, Claudine might easily have grown to adore Mathilde as Annie had.

But then why did she turn her back on the older woman now, in time of need? Was it some kind of penance, to atone for having betrayed her parents by consorting with the enemy? If she was all that loyal to Alice and Claude, could she ever have fallen for Mathilde's charm in the first place? Holly could more easily picture a bitter young Claudine pelting Jonathan's second wife with rotten apples from behind a hedge.

Holly'd been pleased to see Geoffrey, now she wished he'd go away. She wanted to talk with Claudine, to see if she could possibly find out what went on inside that exquisitely polished shell. It didn't look as if she'd get the chance, though. Maybe Geoffrey thought he could wear Claudine down if he stuck around long enough. Anyway, he was still there, wandering around the shop pretending to look at things he couldn't possibly care two hoots about.

Claudine, having spoken her piece, paid no more attention to him. She started talking to Holly in that calm, sure voice about the groceries.

"Annie told me you needed cleaning stuff. I got some scouring powder that was on sale, and a jug of bleach and one of ammonia. I presume you know better than to mix them together."

"Yes," Holly told her. "My roommate did it once and almost gassed us both."

"You were lucky she didn't succeed," Cawne put in. "That's a dangerous combination."

Claudine didn't appear to have heard him. "You asked for fruit and salad greens. I got you a head of lettuce and some ripe tomatoes, and I'll send up a half-peck of apples by Bert as soon as they come in from the orchard. That's the best I can do on what Earl gives me to spend. If you want more, it'll have to come out of your wages."

"That's all right," said Holly. "Thanks very much."

Claudine thawed a little. "Annie told me how you cleaned the bedroom. She says you even took down the draperies and washed the windows. That was a lot to do in one day."

"Too much," Holly agreed. "That's why my leg started acting up. Anyway, I hope Mrs. Parlett's more comfortable. It's not that Annie was neglecting her. She does a fantastic job, considering."

"Does she use the best sheets?" Claudine asked sharply.

Holly flared up. "Why not? They might as well be on the bed as rotting away in the linen closet. Yes, Annie keeps Mrs. Parlett just the way she ought to be: lace-trimmed pillow cases, fancy silk nightgowns, and all."

Even though that handsome face didn't twitch a muscle, Holly knew Claudine was pleased rather than annoyed by her answer. Curiouser and curiouser. Between Claudine and the restlessly prowling Geoffrey, Holly began to grow restive. Ellis, she suddenly realized, had vanished. She hadn't the faintest idea how long he'd been gone.

"When's Bert supposed to be here?" she asked.

Claudine shrugged. "Sooner or later."

Maybe this was the opportunity Geoffrey Cawne had been waiting for. "Holly, I'm on my way home," he said. "Would it help if I ran you as far as Howe Hill?"

"It would be marvelous. Fan was wishing we could have time to visit a little. I'm sure she'll be willing to drive me to Cliff House later on. Is that all right, Claudine?"

"Yes, go ahead. The change might do you good. You will be back before dark, though?"

She's scared, Holly realized. And so am I. Now was her chance to reply, "I'm sorry, Claudine, I've changed my mind. I'm not going back at all."

What she said was, "Don't worry, Claudine. I'll be there."

Chapter 19

"She's a strange woman." Geoffrey spoke without taking his eyes off the road. He was a more careful driver than the racy lines of his gray Jaguar had led Holly to expect.

"Yes, isn't she?" Holly agreed. "Can you tell me why a woman with Claudine's looks and ability hangs around Jugtown nursing the family grudge?"

"Does she? I suppose she is rather good-looking, now that you mention it. I don't quite fancy the type, myself. She looks like your typical Dean of Women. Why do you say ability?"

"Because of the way she keeps her shop. And she couldn't dress like that by accident. I'd say Claudine could be a success anywhere, yet here she sticks."

"Some sort of neurotic fixation, would you say?"

"I wouldn't know about that, but from what Annie Blodgett tells me, I expect she's entitled to one."

Since most of the Jugtowners must know it already, Holly saw no harm in giving Geoffrey a quick rundown of what she'd learned about the Parletts.

"Interesting," he said, not sounding very interested. "But quite frankly, I'd rather hear more about you. I wish there were a place around here I could invite you for a drink. My housekeeper would be shocked if I asked you to the house, I'm afraid."

"I don't drink anyway," Holly told him. "It's fattening and bad for the complexion. Besides, I've just had a gallon or so of antibiotic pumped into me."

"Oh, so that's why you came down? To see the doctor?"

"Yes, one of my cuts was acting up."

"You've been doing too much at Cliff House, no doubt. You'd better take it easy. Have you something for the pain?"

"He gave me a prescription."

"Oh, should we have stopped at the drugstore?"

"I got it filled before I went to Claudine's." Holly yawned. "Sorry, penicillin always makes me drowsy."

"You'll sleep well tonight, then."

"Like a rock, I expect. There's Fan. She'll be surprised to see me with you."

Fan was out in the yard, pouring more oil into her truck. There was a greasy puddle under it already. Was there another vehicle in Jugtown that leaked oil fast enough to leave the sort of stain Holly and Sam Neill had found on the ledge? Had Sam been asking himself the same question? Holly was relieved she didn't have to face him beside those telltale blobs.

"What are you doing here?" was Fan's amiable greeting. She'd switched moods fast enough. Were she and Roger having a fight? Rather, had Fan been fighting with Roger? She did lash out at him sometimes. Roger never bothered to reply, but stalked off to his workshop leaving her to simmer down into her accustomed mold of uncritical worship.

"I came because you said you'd like to visit." Holly felt none too sweet herself, getting this brush-off in front of Geoffrey Cawne.

"I don't have time now. Roger wants me to—do an errand for him."

Cawne stepped gracefully into the breach. "Then why don't I take Holly on out to Cliff House? I do have to keep on her good side, you know, or risk losing my—what is it? My prop girl."

That joggled Holly's memory about the scrapbook. This might be the only chance she'd have to get a look at it. "Would you mind terribly if I ran into the house for a minute? I'd like to pick up a few things from my room."

"Go right ahead. I'll stroll over and check on that antique lathe, if Howe doesn't mind being disturbed."

"Why should he?" said Fan. "He doesn't care how much he disturbs everybody else." But she waited to add that till Cawne was out of earshot. "Come on, Holly, I'll get the stuff for you. You'd better not climb the stairs. What do you want?"

"What I'd really like is a quick peek at your scrapbook."

"For Pete's sake, why?"

Holly shrugged. "Getting antique-minded, I guess. Mainly, I want to show Geoffrey how smart I am."

"Huh! Men don't want smart women, they want willing slaves. Besides, it's not here. I—uh—took it to Saint John to have another copy made, that I'm going to put in a safe-deposit box. What if we should have a fire or something?"

That wasn't a very good lie. Fan would never have left her precious book in strange hands. And why should she? She'd mentioned taking Mrs. Brown's notes to one of those instant Xerox places in the city. They could have reproduced the whole book in about ten minutes. Considering that she'd practically been following Holly around with the thing a week ago, why was she acting so coy all of a sudden?

Holly knew better than to ask. Besides, she mustn't keep Geoffrey waiting. All she could say was, "That's a good idea, Fan," and grab some clean pajamas she didn't particularly need to take with her.

By the time they were on the road to Cliff House, Holly felt too tired for small talk. She leaned her head back against the rich leather upholstery and closed her eyes. After a while, Cawne said, "Mrs. Blodgett won't expect you to work this weekend, I trust?"

"Oh no. Annie's a natural-born mother hen. I'm only afraid she'll try to feed me porridge."

"Good Lord, not that! Tell her Dr. Cawne prescribed tea and toast and plenty of bed rest. And don't forget to take your medication. We want you in shape for another photography session Monday, God and Earl Stoodley willing."

Holly smiled but didn't answer. When they got to Cliff House, she had just about strength enough left to thank him, then stumble up to Cousin Edith's room and collapse on the bed.

She didn't know how long she'd been asleep when Annie bent over her. "You coming down to supper, dearie, or would you like something on a tray?"

"Ungh? Oh, I'll come. Where's Bert?"

"Down by the stove claiming his belly's touching his back-bone. Don't you fret about Bert, dearie. Take your time."

Holly freshened up a little, then picked her way down to the kitchen favoring her bad leg. A more peculiar smell than usual was emanating from the hired man's direction.

"Bert," she demanded, "what on earth are you drinking? Gin and molasses? Oh, I know, rum."

"Ayuh. Claudine sent up a jar for a change. Want a snort?"

"I wouldn't touch it if you paid me."

Annie had her share, though, while Holly fixed herself a salad of lettuce and tomatoes. That and canned baked beans made an adequate meal. There was greasy fried bacon, too, but she skipped that. For dessert, Bert and Annie had another taste of Claudine's rum, then they both went to sleep in their chairs. Holly stretched out on the cot in the corner with one of those library books she hadn't yet got around to reading but hadn't turned more than five pages before she herself fell asleep.

She woke stiff and cramped, and no wonder. According to the kitchen clock it was well past midnight. She'd been sleeping almost six hours. Bert and Annie were still in their chairs, too. Holly shook Annie's shoulder gently, but the housekeeper only grunted and kept on snoring.

Now what? She couldn't possibly budge either of these dead weights. She mustn't even try, for fear of putting more strain on her bad leg. She settled for shoving another stick of wood into the stove and getting a couple of afghans to tuck the two up as best she could. This probably wasn't the first time they'd slept off a Saturday night party here by the stove.

She might as well go to bed herself, Holly supposed, but she didn't feel sleepy now. Besides, the fuggy odors of bacon fat, wood smoke, and Bert were making her queasy. What she needed was a breath of fresh air. Late as it was, Holly wrapped Annie's old black shawl around her and stepped outside.

The air was warmer than she'd expected, soft and misty and tasting of salt. Were they in for a rainstorm? There wasn't a star to be seen, but she could make out her way across the yard to the stone wall that marked its boundary. To venture beyond that point would be foolhardy. One false step could send her rolling down the hillside to the cliff. If the tide happened to be on the make, she'd drown before anybody knew she'd fallen.

Holly sat down on a low stone with another for a backrest. It was good to be alone for a change. Or was she? Were those footsteps she heard coming along the terrace?

Quickly Holly hugged her body into a tight ball and pulled the shawl around her, head and all. Could this be Annie's ghost? It wasn't Bert or Annie, anyway. The steps were too quick and firm, too far apart. It must be somebody tall and vigorous, somebody she was in no shape to tangle with.

Her sore leg began to ache from being squeezed so tight against her body. She felt suffocated inside her cocoon of wool; still she didn't dare move. The prowler was close to her now, maybe wondering if that odd bulge was really another rock, maybe debating whether this was a safe time to enter Cliff House.

Oh, God! She'd left the kitchen door on the latch and those two old people asleep inside. All he had to do was turn the knob and—why did it have to be a he? Plenty of women had firm, long-legged strides. She did herself, when her legs were working right. Fan wasn't tall, but she thundered along like a charging bison. Claudine Parlett was no pigmy, and what about the mysterious Mrs. Brown?

The temptation to raise her head and take a peek was almost harder to endure than the agony in her leg. Yet she stayed motionless until, mercifully, the footsteps began to move away. She could hear a rattle of pebbles as the intruder climbed over the wall only a few feet from where she crouched, and headed down over the hill.

She moved now, because she had to. If she didn't ease the pressure on that cut, she'd surely scream from the pain and betray herself. Inch by inch, keeping the shawl over her head for camouflage, Holly rolled over on her knees, raised her eyes above the wall, and looked through the meshes of the crocheted wool.

Yes, there he was, almost certainly a man and a big one, not trying to hide himself because he wouldn't think anybody was looking. He appeared to be concentrating on something out in the bay, but what? Holly couldn't see anything except that tiny speck of phosphorescence that marked Ellis Parlett's phony lobster trap.

All of a sudden, the buoy began to jerk. Something must be jiggling the line to which it was tied, but why? Could a fish be interested in a big old chest of drawers?

Drawers! Holly almost made the serious mistake of gasping aloud. Now she knew why Ellis Parlett anchored his fake antiques in such an unlikely place. Now she knew why somebody had rowed out there last night in the dark and gone through that apparently senseless performance of hauling up the dresser and letting it down again. He'd been putting something in the drawers. Now a scuba diver was down in that inky, treacherous water taking it out.

Crazy? Not really. All up and down the Atlantic coast, smugglers had been plying their illegal trade ever since the first royal revenue inspector set foot on New World shores. The international boundary line wasn't all that far from here. No matter how efficient the Coast Guard might be, how could they possibly cover all the shore, all the time? Even in daylight such a task would be impossible. How much less apt would anyone be to spot a diver in a black wetsuit swimming out there in the dark?

The buoy wasn't jerking any more. The diver must have got what he wanted and be heading—where? Back to shore, most likely. Or so the watcher on the hill must be thinking. Holly could make him out moving slowly downward, feeling ahead for any twig or stone that might betray him. He couldn't be meeting the diver, she thought. He must think a second person was waiting below, and was spying to find out who it could be.

At least it wouldn't be anybody in a leaky old truck on the ledge, not tonight. That makeshift road would be under twenty feet of water about now. There'd be a boat hidden under the overhang of the cliff, Holly thought, but not necessarily a boatman. The diver could have left one there himself, tied to a rock or hauled into one of those caves Sam Neill had pointed out to her.

After the tide had made its phenomenal inward surge, it didn't suddenly suck itself backward but receded gradually like any other tide. The boatman could row quite a way under the shelter of the cliff, then hide his boat somewhere else and make a dash for a waiting car, or else meet a yacht anchored well away from Parlett's Point and be hauled aboard.

But why such an elaborate setup? Diving at night in a place like this must be risky even for a professional. Why not just row out and pull up the chest as that other person had done?

Because there was always the chance some camper, or a pair of lovers, or a wakeful woman at Cliff House might see you doing it. Holly had a feeling this was no amateur prank, but a well-organized professional operation. That meant the stakes would be high enough to make the danger worthwhile.

Maybe that person in the rowboat last night hadn't been part of it, but some local who'd got to wondering about Ellis Parlett's so-called lobster traps and come to take a look out of curiosity. That would explain the watcher on the hill. He'd found something and was now trying to find out who'd come after it.

And maybe he wasn't just an idle onlooker but a rival smuggler. She'd be crazy to stay out here another second. He'd be coming back this way, most likely. Bending low and keeping the shawl over her like a tent, Holly made a beeline for the kitchen. The temptation to slam the back door behind her was great, but she managed somehow to ease it shut and thrust home the bolt without making a sound.

Bert lay sprawled on the iron cot now with the afghan wadded around his neck, but Annie was gone. She must have roused herself and put herself decently to bed. Good. Holly kicked her sodden slippers under the stove and padded barefoot through the now familiar dark house. She'd be inviting trouble if she showed a light and let that person out there know the household was stirring.

Annie's door was wide open tonight. The old woman lay on her bed fully clothed, emitting muffled snorts. Holly managed to get her cardigan and housedress off and bundle the covers over her. Then she went back to her own room. From there she could see the jug in the water and the wall behind which she'd lurked. Thank goodness she'd come in when she did. The night prowler was back on the terrace, standing in almost the identical spot where she'd done her impersonation of a rock.

Could the man possibly be as tall as he looked in that gray mist? Why not? There were plenty of long-boned males in the area, men like Sam Neill and her own brother Roger. Earl Stoodley was a big man, too, but fatter than this one. At least Geoffrey Cawne was out of the running. He'd be too short. It couldn't be Sam either, come to think of it, because Sam was down in Saint John with his sick mother.

Or was he? Bert's saying Sam had gone didn't mean he'd stayed. Bert wouldn't know. He must have been up here working on Claudine's jar half the afternoon, judging from the state he was in now. The longer Holly watched, the more she got the uncomfortable feeling this could be Sam. He had the sure, vigorous way of moving. He knew the terrain. But why should Sam be putting on this cloak-and-dagger act?

What would happen if she stuck her head out the window and called to him? What would happen if it wasn't Sam after all, or if Sam wasn't the sort of man she thought he was?

Whoever he was, he moved. She wondered in sudden panic whether he meant to force his way into the house. No, he'd merged into the dense shrubbery that lined the overgrown drive. He was going down to the road. Nothing more would happen now. And Holly Howe would be dead on her feet if she didn't get a few more hours' sleep before she had to face another day at Cliff House.

Chapter 20

About half-past seven, Holly was awakened by sounds of distress from the bathroom. "Annie," she called, "what's the matter?"

"Oh dearie, I'm poorly."

That was a masterpiece of understatement. The poor old soul was retching so violently she hadn't the strength to stand. Holly did her best, supporting the flaccid body, bathing the sweating face with a damp washcloth, helping Annie back to her own room. She got her into a clean nightgown, put her back to bed, and covered her with extra blankets. Annie lay there shivering, her eyes sunk into wrinkled black pools. Holly would have been frantic if she hadn't known about the rum.

"I don't know when I've felt so bad," Annie whispered.

"Do you want me to call Dr. Walker?"

"No dearie, don't do that. I'll be all right in a while."

That was probably true. Now that she'd got the alcohol out of her system, rest and a hot water bottle should be cure enough. Holly gave Annie a comforting pat and went down to boil a kettle. She'd been afraid she might find Bert in equally bad shape, but all those years of training must have toughened his resistance. He was on his legs and mending the fire, cursing with almost half his usual fluency.

"Well, I see you're bright-eyed and bushytailed," Holly remarked.

"Ungh. How's Annie?"

"Poorly. Hand me that kettle, will you? I'm trying to get her warm."

Bert passed over the teakettle with an air of outraged virtue. "Ain't nothin' more disgustin' than a drunken woman."

"Then what did you get her sloshed for?"

"Quit yellin', can't you? Cripes, if a field mouse was to back into a pussywillow just now, I don't think I could stand the noise o' the collision."

Bert slumped into the rocking chair and glowered at the oven door. Holly put the coffeepot on, fixed Annie's hot water bottle from the teakettle, and took it upstairs.

Annie's eyes were shut, but she whispered, "That you, dearie? I don't know how I'm going to drag myself out to get her breakfast. Just the look of porridge would set me off again."

Holly'd forgotten there was another invalid to feed and clean up. "Never mind, Annie," she sighed. "I'll do it as soon as I get the porridge boiled. That's what she has, isn't it?"

"That's right, dearie. Porridge and tea. Ugh!"

Annie groaned but mercifully didn't start retching again. Holly put the comforting heat to the old woman's stomach and went back to her own room to change into jeans and a sweatshirt. When she got down to the kitchen again, Bert had dozed off and the coffeepot was boiling over. She shoved it to the back of the stove and poured herself a mug to sip while she stirred the porridge.

At last it began to plop tiny volcanoes that sent scalding spatters over her hand. She mustn't let the gruel get too thick or Mrs. Parlett wouldn't be able to swallow it. She mustn't allow any lumps to form or Mrs. Parlett might choke. She must get up there and do what she had to, much as she disliked the thought.

Propping up that all-but-lifeless body was like handling a puppet. When it came to poking food into the silent mouth, Holly almost panicked. Eating seemed to be the one physical act Mrs. Parlett could still perform with any sign of intelligence, though. If Holly was late with the next spoonful, her mouth would hang open in reproachful expectation, bits of porridge clinging to the mucous membrane. When the last scrape of gruel, the last sip of tea had disappeared, the mouth closed and stayed closed.

Was it mere instinct, or did a spark of awareness linger in that worn-out frame? Did she know what had become of her, the laughing Mathilde who'd gathered field flowers to brighten the dark corners of Cliff House? Now Holly understood why Annie kept on laundering the lace-edged pillowcases and the delicate nightgowns.

"I'll pick you some flowers as soon as I get a chance," Holly promised. "You'll like that, won't you? Now I'm going to get you fixed up nice and comfortable."

That was the sort of thing Annie would say. Holly'd heard her droning on to Mathilde often enough. The words didn't matter, it was the love in the voice that counted. She carried the tray out and was on her way to the bathroom for warm water and towels when the phone rang. It was Geoffrey, wondering if she'd be free to work with him that morning.

"I can't," Holly wailed. "Annie's sick in bed and I've got both her and Mrs. Parlett to look after. Anyway, Earl Stoodley wouldn't want to come on a Sunday."

"I've just spent twenty minutes talking him into it." Geoffrey sounded rather frosty. "What's the matter with Annie?"

"A gastric upset." That was close enough to the truth.

"Do you think it's anything catching?"

"Oh no, I'm quite sure it's not."

"Then we may as well come. If you can't help me, I'll have to muddle along as best I can. Would it be possible for you to take time out from your nursing to open the door for us?"

"I expect I can manage that much."

Holly waited till he'd rung off before she slammed down the receiver. Of all the things she didn't need today, this had to be number one!

She got the basin and towels and went back to Mrs. Parlett, trying to remember how to do a back rub. Was it alcohol or talcum powder you used? Alcohol dried the skin, but powder might make the patient sneeze and choke. She went to ask Annie and found her asleep, curled around the hot water bottle. She'd skip the alcohol. There'd been too much of it used around here already.

To Holly's surprise, she found she didn't mind coping with the pathetic effects of incontinence. What got to her was the simple act of bending over to change Mrs. Parlett's bed. The muscles in her injured thigh pulled till the whole leg felt as if it were on fire. By the time Geoffrey Cawne and his portly bodyguard arrived, she didn't see how she could manage to descend that long flight of stairs and let them in. Holly solved that problem by sliding down the bannisters.

"What's the matter with Annie?" was Earl Stoodley's greeting.

Holly's leg gave her a nasty twinge. She snapped back, "Mostly I think she's plain exhausted. You have no idea how tough it is to take care of Mrs. Parlett without proper facilities. Couldn't you at least rent a hospital bed so we wouldn't have to do so much bending?"

"Far's I know, nobody's standing over you with a blacksnake whip," he replied blandly.

"What's that supposed to mean, that we let her lie there and starve to death in her own filth? This is still Mrs. Parlett's house and it's her money that pays us, in case you've forgotten."

"I'm not one to forget anything. S'pose you try to remember whether it's her or me who does the hiring and firing around here."

Holly caught a warning glance from Geoffrey and didn't answer back. With Annie too ill to cope, Stoodley would adore an excuse to fire the new helper on the spot and let Mrs. Parlett die of neglect. Should Annie happen to die, too, he'd just blame Holly for having deserted two helpless invalids, and set happily about making his own dream of glory come true. She turned and went down to the laundry room with her burden of reeking sheets.

When she'd set the old-fashioned washing machine thumping and bumping, she hauled herself back to the kitchen. She should have warned Bert visitors were coming. A glance told her she needn't have worried. Bert was too wily an old fox to be caught by Earl Stoodley. He'd even smoothed out the cot where he'd slept, and folded the afghan. Only a few extra dishes in the sink and a lingering mephitic whiff betrayed the fact that he'd been there. An opened window and a dishpan full of hot suds took care of those clues. Holly was innocently stacking away clean china when the two men came to find her.

"I hate to disturb you," Geoffrey apologized, "but could you spare two minutes to give us your opinion of this setup?"

"Certainly." She hung up her cup towel and followed him to the back parlor. For an amateur he hadn't done badly, though the group he'd assembled was curiously assorted. Early pie-crust tables flanked a late Victorian loveseat. Matching Sèvres urns on the tables made a strange contrast to gaudy Berlin-work sofa pillows and a silly Art Deco doll Mathilde must have picked up in Paris.

"My idea was to show the mélange of treasures spanning the centuries," Cawne explained. "Is it too much of a hodge-podge?"

"No, I think it's fun," Holly told him. "I'm just wondering how you'll get it all in without distortion."

"I thought I'd use my wide-angle lens. Would you care to look through the view-finder? You'll have to climb up on this footstool. I thought a high angle would be better, to pick up the carving on the loveseat and those nice finials on the urns."

Stifling a groan, Holly did as he asked. "The angle isn't bad, but your lighting is too flat. You'll wash out the detail. Move your left-hand flood about eight inches—no, that's no good. You've picked up a glare from the table top."

"Those tables are a problem. The wood's so highly polished it acts like a mirror."

So it did. The last time Holly'd noticed those tables, they'd been coated with dust and grime. That must have been Thursday, the last time she'd helped Geoffrey. She remembered bumping into one and noticing a chip out of its edge while she was hunting for props to use with that ill-chosen Bible box. The edge wasn't chipped now. Both tables looked good as new. And that same night she'd been locked into this room.

And only yesterday Fan had remarked that they'd got that pair of piecrust tables shipped off to Mrs. Brown.

Cawne was getting restless. "What's the matter, Holly? Is the lighting still wrong?"

"Do you have to use those tables?" Her voice was too shrill.

"Why not?" he said in some surprise. "Go ahead, if they're wrong, say so. Don't worry about hurting my feelings, what matters is that we make no mistakes. My distinguished colleagues will be going over every page with a magnifying glass, and if there's any fault to be found, I assure you they'll find it."

Lovely! And Geoffrey was also going to include illustrations of local artisan Roger Howe with his eighteenth-century tools and his foot-powered lathe. Once the fakes were spotted, it wouldn't take a university professor to figure out who was responsible for them.

"The tables are no good," Holly said flatly.

"No good?" sputtered Earl Stoodley. "They're worth thousands and thousands of dollars."

"I don't mean that. I mean they—they're out of proportion to that heavy loveseat."

"Then let's take away the loveseat and just show the tables," said Geoffrey.

"That's stupid! It destroys your whole concept. You can't just have two dinky little tables sitting side by side."

His eyebrows shot up, and no wonder. She'd been yelling. Earl Stoodley was watching with a strangely blank look on his pudgy face. With a supreme effort, Holly pulled herself together.

"Look, why don't we do it this way? Pull the loveseat around at a right angle to the fireplace, leave the doll and pillows as they are, and set the urns on the mantelpiece. The

Chippendale firescreen and the brass warming pan can go side by side opposite the loveseat and I'll bring down a marvelous Victorian paper fan out of the fireplace in my bedroom. That gets in more contrast of periods with greater design interest. If you're absolutely hung up on those tables, we can set one at the end of the loveseat next to the fireplace."

Where it would be almost totally hidden, as Stoodley was quick to point out. "Why not drag it out where folks can see it?"

"Because that's not good photographic layout," Holly argued. "You don't line things up in a row like bowling pins. Please try it my way. If you don't like the layout, we can always come back to this one."

In a pig's eye they could. By the time she got through shoving things around, they'd have forgotten all about the piecrust tables. Holly'd done enough camera work to know how fast an original concept can get lost in the shuffle. Furthermore, she was hoping Earl would start wanting his Sunday dinner pretty soon.

Her stratagem worked, but her leg took a terrible beating. By the time she'd limped upstairs for props, helped Cawne move the furniture and rearrange the lighting, she was half out of her mind with pain. Still, she'd produced a handsome layout and maybe saved her brother's neck.

On the other hand, she'd probably cooked her goose with Geoffrey by criticizing him in front of Earl Stoodley, and she'd been away from her patients too long. As soon as they'd finished shooting she said, "I'm sorry, but I've got to go now. Mrs. Parlett should have been fed at noon and it's almost one o'clock."

Cawne began to apologize, but Stoodley cut him short. "Don't let that bother you, Professor. I guess she's learning to put first things first around here."

Holly felt her face blaze and her throat tighten, but this time she had sense enough to keep quiet. She couldn't fight Earl Stoodley with words.

Chapter 21

"Annie, do please take a sip of tea. You've got to get something into your stomach or you'll dehydrate."

The housekeeper was proving a more difficult patient than Mrs. Parlett. It was suppertime now, and Holly was ready to push the panic button. She'd half-dragged Annie to the bathroom a couple of times during the afternoon, but now Annie was so weak that she couldn't get out of bed at all. Still she insisted she wouldn't have the doctor.

"Come on, try," Holly begged again.

This time, Annie allowed a few drops to pass between her blue lips. "Thank you, dearie," she whispered. "That's enough."

"No it isn't. Drink some more." Wheedling, scolding, threatening to call Dr. Walker, Holly managed to get about half a cup of tea into the old woman. Miraculously, it stayed down. "There, see. You're doing fine."

"Yes, dearie." The voice was a mere thread of sound. The gray head lolled back on the pillow.

"Oh my God," Holly thought, "she's dead." She actually fetched a mirror and held it to Annie's mouth to convince herself Annie was still breathing.

Now she couldn't fool around any longer. At least she could call Claudine. Since it was Claudine who'd sent up the rum, she didn't pussyfoot about what was wrong with Annie, and Claudine was every bit as upset as she should have been.

"Poor Annie, she has so few pleasures. I ought to have known better, with that old souse Bert egging her on. No, please don't call the doctor. If Annie's no better in the morning I'll get someone to bring her down here. Now that you've managed to get something into her, though, I expect she'll be all right. How are you managing with Mrs. Parlett?"

"Oh, she's an old sweetie," Holly said. "That's like taking care of a baby who never cries. I'm growing fond of her."

"Are you really, Holly? That's—I'm glad. Call me again if you're worried. Any time, night or day."

Holly could swear Claudine was crying when she hung up, but she had no time to wonder why. There was still Mrs. Parlett's supper to take up, and loud clanking from the drive told her Bert Walker was arriving. She hobbled out to meet him.

"Oh Bert, I'm so glad to see you. I hope you're not expecting a proper Sunday meal, though. You'll be lucky to get another can of beans tonight."

"I've et worse. What's the matter? Where's Annie?"

"Still in bed. She's been sick as a dog all day. I'm worried about her, Bert."

"Did you call Ben?"

"Dr. Walker? She wouldn't let me."

"Stands to reason. She wouldn't want him to know what made 'er sick." The prunelike face split in an evil grin.

"That's not funny," Holly snapped. "Honestly, Bert, a little while ago I thought she was dead."

"Hell's bells, you couldn't kill Annie Blodgett with a shotgun. She's tough, like me." Nevertheless Bert began to look worried. "No foolin', Holly, is she that bad off?"

"I wouldn't have believed a person could get that sick from a few drinks of rum and water. She didn't eat something that could have given her food poisoning?"

"Far's I know, she only et what we did. Didn't bother you none, did it?"

"No, I was all right as far as that went. How about you?"

"My guts was kind o' queasy this mornin' an' my eyeballs felt as if somebody was tryin' to gouge 'em out with a dirty

fingernail, but that went away once I'd swilled down a bucket
or two o' black coffee."

He ruminated awhile, working his stubbled jaws back and
forth. "Know what I think? I seen this same thing happen once
up in the Yukon. A Mountie'd trailed a crazy trapper single-
handed in the dead o' winter an' brought 'im out by dogsled to
a minin' camp where he found everybody down with some
pestilence or other, me included. Cripes, I was never so sick in
my life. The Mountie was wore out hisself by then, but he
nursed the whole bunch till a few of us was well enough to
take care o' the rest. Then him an' me set out for Stillwater to
turn over the prisoner an' get help for the camp. I never seen a
man so tuckered out as that Mountie, but he hung to it till we
got there. Once he'd made 'is report, he folded up like a wet
dishrag. They had to tilt up his head an' spoon hot brandy into
'im to get his eyes open. He wasn't sick, only plumb used up."

"You could be right," said Holly. "Annie's been here alone
far too long. I've had one day of it and I'm beat to the socks already." She sank into a chair and propped her sore leg up on
the oven ledge. "How long did it take the Mountie to re-
cover?"

"I don't know. I went back with the rescue team to show
'em the trail. Cripes, what a trip that was!"

Bert launched into another of his interminable reminis-
cences. Holly let him talk, knowing it didn't matter whether
she listened. Bert was telling the story to himself, reminding
himself that he'd once been as strong as the best, pulling a
man's weight in a world not made for weaklings. It was the
strong who survived. Annie was tough. She'd make it. Feeling
a little better, Holly got up to fix supper.

Bert broke off his tale to remark, "Annie always offers me a
hair of the dog before we eat."

"I didn't think you'd want one, after last night."

"Hell, that was last night."

"Then do me a favor and stay away from the rum. I don't

even want to smell it. There's about one good belt left in the whiskey bottle."

Bert grumbled, but he condescended to accept the glass Holly gave him. "I s'pose I'll have to bring up another jar tomorrow if you're goin' to be so blamed stingy with Claudine's."

"I'm not being stingy, I just don't want another living corpse on my hands. I'll pay for your jar if it makes you any happier."

"'Twon't hurt my feelin's none." He took a swig. "Ah, that's the stuff for what ails you. Why don't you take a little nip to Annie?"

"Because I don't want to kill her, that's why. Haul up your chair."

Baked beans on toast with a few fried eggs and a handful of store cookies, washed down with every drop he could wring from the whiskey bottle and a quart or so of strong tea satisfied Bert nicely. He scorned Holly's offer of salad.

"That stuff's for rabbits. Gimme a few more beans if you got 'em handy."

"I don't know where you put it all," Holly marveled.

The hired man had no more spare flesh on his bones than a picked crow, yet he ate enough to satisfy three ordinary appetites. Now that Holly's yoghurt and carrot stick days were over, she wasn't doing so badly at the table herself. It was a long jump from Seventh Avenue to Parlett's Point. Who'd have thought she'd ever wind up sitting around a well-scrubbed oilcloth with a totally unscrubbed old reprobate, wondering if she had strength enough left to put that last load of wet sheets through the wringer?

To heck with the sheets. There were still some clean ones upstairs even though she'd had to remake both her patients' beds twice so far. She went up to check on Annie, carrying a cup of tea with her. Remembering Bert's tale of the Mountie, she simply tilted the housekeeper's head up and put the cup to her lips.

"Drink it or I'll pour it down your neck."

Annie began to swallow. Holly made her empty the cup, then went back to Bert.

"I got a whole cup of tea into her," she told him with satisfaction. "She's still pretty feeble, but her color's better than it was."

"Glad to hear it," he grunted. "She'll be back on 'er feet in a day or two."

"I hope my feet last that long."

Holly sat down again. Bert, in one of his unexpected bursts of gallantry, went and got some extra cushions so she could rest in comfort.

"Thanks, Bert, that does feel better. I took some aspirin while I was upstairs. Maybe that'll quiet this thing down for a while."

"Women are always dosin' themselves," he snorted. "Only one medicine ever done me any good."

"Bert, if you're angling for another drink, forget it. I won't have you passing out on me again tonight. Say something bright and witty."

"You tryin' to make fun o' me?"

"I shouldn't dream of it," Holly assured him. "All right, if you won't be funny, let's talk shop. How's it going at Howe Hill?"

"'Bout the same as usual."

"Don't be ornery. Tell me things."

"What sort o' things?"

"Well, for instance, how do they handle the shipping?"

"Him an' me crates it up, then she takes it down to Saint John."

"You mean to say Fan delivers the furniture all by herself?"

"Not to say delivers it. As I understand it, she takes the crates to a shippin' warehouse an' they handle it from there."

"I see," said Holly with a sinking heart. "What warehouse?"

"Don't ask me. 'Tain't none o' my business. That Miz Brown makes all the arrangements, sends 'em the customs' forms an' whatnot. Miz Howe, she does all the paperwork an' Roger makes the crates hisself. Spends as much time on the crates as he does on the furniture, a'most. Way he fits 'em an' pads 'em, you'd think he was cratin' a baby."

"I suppose in a sense his creations are his children," said Holly. "I've never thought of them that way before. To be honest with you, I've seldom thought about my brother at all, until lately."

"There's times I don't think much of 'im, myself, if you want the honest truth. Any man that would let 'is wife go off alone in the dead o' night drivin' that wreck of a truck an' sleepin' alongside the road—"

"Bert, is that really what Fan does?"

"Yep. She gets Roger's supper, then sets the table for his breakfast, an' starts off all sole alone in the dark. She drives till she gets too sleepy to go any farther, then she pulls off somewheres an' grabs forty winks, goes on an' gets to the warehouse soon as it opens, about ha'past seven in the mornin'. The men there unload for her, then she gets reckless an' selfish an' splurges on a cup o' coffee. After that she heads for home worryin' for fear she won't be there in time to get Roger's dinner an' he might have to spread hisself a piece o' bread an' butter."

Bert spat into the stove. Holly asked no more questions. She'd already learned more than she wanted to know. Once Roger's work was out of the shop, Fan was free to take it anywhere she chose. She could simply pretend to start for Saint John, drive out here under cover of darkness, break into Cliff House as she'd broken into so many others, and switch the reproduction for the original.

Opening the crate and switching Roger's nameplate wouldn't take long. Small pieces like the Bible box and the piecrust tables would be easy for her to manage alone. Fan wouldn't have to risk that perilous road along the ledge, just park within walking distance and carry the furniture back and forth. It was only big pieces like that Sheraton highboy Roger and Sam were now working on that would have to be hauled over the cliff. For that she'd need help, but there must be at least one other person involved in this racket anyway. Fan simply didn't have what it took to manage a swindle of such magnitude on her own.

Getting the stolen merchandise through customs would be no great problem. The original could be passed off as an authentic Roger Howe reproduction, with its little brass nameplate attached and all its papers filled out in good order. Was Fan really doing this, and did Roger know? His sending her off alone at night in a broken-down truck didn't mean anything. He'd send her across the Grand Canyon on a tightrope if he happened to want a box of nails from the other side.

"You asleep?"

Holly jumped. She'd been so wrapped up in her thoughts, she'd forgotten Bert was there. "I'm sorry," she told him. "That aspirin must be putting me to sleep."

"Time I went along, then." He got up and headed for the door. "Guess I'll turn in early myself. It's lonesome down there with nobody home. By the way, Sam called from Saint John. Says his mother's doin' fine, an' he'll be back tomorrow."

"That's nice," said Holly.

But how did Bert know Sam really had called from Saint John? Or rather, how long had Sam been there? If Fan could make the trip overnight in that rattletrap of hers, Sam's shiny new wagon ought to do it in half the time. Remembering that man who'd come so close to stepping on her in the yard last night, Holly had an uneasy feeling she'd better not make the mistake of trusting Sam Neill too far.

Chapter 22

Dr. Walker's medicine must be working. Despite her hectic day, Holly slept well and woke on Monday with her leg less inflamed. She treated herself to a therapeutic dunk in her beloved zinc tub, then went to check on her patients.

"Hi, Annie. How are you feeling?"

"Hello, dearie." That seemed to be as far as Annie cared to go at the moment. Holly left her to feed Mrs. Parlett. When she got back half an hour later, Annie hadn't stirred.

"Would you like me to help you to the bathroom?" she asked.

"No, dearie."

"How about sitting on the pot?"

"Yes, dearie."

Sighing as if she begrudged the effort, Annie let Holly help her up on the awkward substitute for the bedpan they didn't have. The procedure was tiring for both of them, but only Annie got to flop back on her bed afterward. Holly had to pick up her armload of dirty sheets and go down to the washing machine.

That tended to, she fixed another tray of tea and porridge. Maybe it was bad psychology to offer Annie the same invalid fare as Mrs. Parlett's, but what else could she do? She took up the tray, propped Annie's head with pillows, and began spooning gruel into her mouth. At this, Annie did rouse herself a bit.

"I'm not that far gone, dearie."

"Then prove it. Let's see you empty this bowl."

Annie managed one or two mouthfuls, then let the spoon drop. "Too much work," she muttered.

"Then you've got to let me feed you. Open up." This time, Holly had a little better success. Annie swallowed another spoonful of porridge and drank most of the tea before she turned her head away.

"All right, you've been a good girl. Now I'm going to wash your face and hands and let you get back to sleep."

After she'd got Annie tidied, Holly went downstairs and fried herself a couple of eggs. She was eating when the phone rang. It was Fan.

"Bert tells me you've got trouble out there. Anything I can do?"

"Thanks, Fan, but we seem to be under control now. Annie's better."

"How about you? All that running up and down stairs can't be doing your leg much good."

"It isn't bothering me, thank goodness. Dr. Walker must know his stuff."

"Well, that's a relief. Let me know if you need to see him again."

"I will. You're sweet to be thinking of me." Holly hung up, wondering. Why had Fan never once mentioned those trips to Saint John? She talked freely enough about everything else that concerned her.

Or did she? A constant flow of words could be a form of noncommunication. By never letting anybody else get a word in, Fan made it impossible to have a real person-to-person exchange. What was it Fan wanted to hide? That she was a swindler, or the tool of one?

Why not think about something easier? For instance, how did the thief get in and out of the house? Earl Stoodley had seen to it there were plenty of locks, and Annie was careful about them, especially since she'd started hearing those noises in the night. Keys alone wouldn't help; there were chains and bolts to be unfastened and refastened afterward, or Annie would surely have noticed. There simply had to be an easy way. Holly put the breakfast dishes to soak, and started hunting.

Cliff House had an amazing number of doors. Holly rattled more chains than Marley's ghost but found no weak link anywhere. Some of the locks looked as if they hadn't been turned in years. Of these she was especially wary, poking at the screws with a knife to make sure they hadn't been loosened.

Doors could also be lifted free of their locks by taking out the hinge pins. She got a screwdriver and hammer and tapped to make sure none of them slipped in and out with suspicious ease. She even used the reading glass to look for telltale scratches but found only a few fresh ones she'd made herself. Earl Stoodley would love her for that.

Windows had to be checked, too. She saw dust lying in furry rows along the tops of sashes; window fasteners corroded so badly they'd never work again. When it came time to renovate Cliff House, the painters would have to unscrew the locks and —and why couldn't she have thought of that before? It didn't take her ten minutes to find a window that could be raised with its dust and its lock intact.

There was nothing supernatural about it. Someone had taken the screws out of the back halves of the catches, reamed out the holes to twice their size, and put back the screws. When the sash was raised from the outside or the inside, the screws simply lifted free. When it was lowered, the screws settled back into their oversized holes. While Annie'd been fussing over all those locks and bolts every night, Cliff House had stayed wide open.

Holly found trick windows in the dining room, the front parlor, Jonathan Parlett's library, and in the room Aunt Maude had perhaps called her conservatory, where overturned flowerpots lay kicked into corners, perhaps by someone hurrying to get another of the family heirlooms out of the house.

Well, the next time the ghost walked, it would be in for a surprise. Holly went down cellar, rummaged among the clutter, and came back with some putty and a handful of screws long enough to hold securely in the reamed-out holes. She made a botch of getting them in and put enough scratches in the woodwork to make Earl Stoodley's heart bleed, but nobody would get through these windows again without having to break the glass.

Probably she ought to get the police up here, but how could she? That would start a hue and cry, and it wouldn't take long for anybody with half a brain to find out about the reproductions. They would lead directly to Roger Howe, and straight back to his sister who was so conveniently on the spot. In more ways than one. She'd better quit detecting and get back to her patients. It was almost noon.

Why hadn't Claudine telephoned to see how Annie was? She'd seemed concerned enough yesterday. Maybe she had, while Holly was down cellar or making too much noise with her hammering to hear the phone. It wouldn't hurt to call the shop, just in case.

Claudine was busy with a customer, or said she was. She listened to Holly's brief report, said, "Let me know if you need anything," and hung up. So much for the bleeding heart department. Chicken soup time again. Holly went into the pantry, stared at the cluster of identical tins, and went back to the phone.

"Claudine, send us some different kinds of soup. Annie hates chicken and so do I."

Without waiting for an answer, Holly hung up. She could do it, too. Feeling absurdly pleased with herself, Holly heated soup for Mrs. Parlett and whipped up an eggnog for Annie.

When she took it up, Annie was awake. "How's it going?" she asked. "Feeling better?"

"Yes, dearie." The voice was still hardly more than a breath.

"That's good. I've brought you an eggnog and I want you to have every drop of it drunk by the time I finish feeding Mrs. Parlett."

"Yes, dearie."

Annie didn't pick up the glass. It would still be sitting on the night stand when Holly got back. She should have asked Claudine to send up some drinking straws, not that they'd do much good. What Annie needed was not just nourishment, but somebody to care that she got it. Holly bent down and kissed the wan cheek.

"You be a good kid. I'll be back soon."

Holly was glad she'd cleaned Mrs. Parlett's room. How had Annie endured sitting day after day in such a dusty, gloomy, smelly place with this heart-wringing scrap of worn-out humanity?

Maybe Annie had still been able to see this room as it was when she'd first come to Cliff House from the tumble-down farm where she'd slept three to a bed with her sisters, crammed in the middle because she was the littlest. That was when Aunt Maude had brought her here to work for her board and keep, treating her not as a person but as a source of cheap labor. Holly was glad it was Mathilde and not Maude she had to care for.

"You'd never do a thing like that, would you?" she crooned.

It seemed impossible Mathilde could understand, yet her eyelids lifted as if in agreement. Holly hadn't noticed before how lovely Mathilde's eyes still were. They were large, of an unusual grayish hazel like clear water running over stones in a brook. Then the lids dropped, ochre-colored rags hiding their beautiful secret. Holly spooned soup until the cup was empty, sponged Mathilde's face and hands, checked her linen, and went back to Annie.

As she'd expected, the eggnog was untouched. She pulled Annie to a half-sitting position, propped her with pillows, and picked up the glass.

"Okay, no more playing games. You're going to drink this if it takes all afternoon."

It did take quite a while, with pauses for swallowing, breath catching, and pep talks when Annie showed signs of wanting to quit, but at last the glass was empty. Then Holly fetched warm water, soap, and towels and proceeded with a bed bath, to Annie's embarrassment.

"It's too much for you, dearie."

"Hush up or I'll get soap in your mouth. How'd you like a back rub?"

"I don't know. I never had one."

"Then it's high time you did. Can you roll over?"

Annie made feeble scrabbling motions. Heartened by this small sign of improvement, Holly heaved her over, sprinkled the age-spotted back with talcum powder, and began to rub. "Feel good?"

"Lovely, dearie."

She's perking up, Holly thought, but Annie was asleep before the back rub was finished. Holly straightened the covers, lowered the blinds, and tiptoed out, taking the dirty dishes with her. It wasn't till she was putting them in the dishpan that she remembered she hadn't had any lunch herself.

There was still a little chicken soup in the pan, but that was the last thing Holly wanted. She made herself a lettuce and to-mato sandwich and took it out to the back terrace. It was good to get out, away from dust and decay and things that had been around too long.

Poor Mathilde, lying up there in her dainty nightgown, with those withered eyelids hiding her beautiful eyes. She must have something fresh and bright to look at, if she ever opened them again. Holly got up and roamed the hillside, picking black-eyed Susans, Queen Anne's lace, and wild asters, divid-ing them scrupulously into two equal piles. It was time Annie, too, knew how it felt to have somebody bring her flowers.

Chapter 23

"My, aren't they pretty!" Food and rest were doing their work. Annie responded to the bouquet like a real, live human being.

"I'll set them here in front of the mirror so they'll look like more," said Holly. "It's rather a sparse arrangement, but they're almost gone by now and I wanted Mrs. Parlett to have some, too. She always liked the wild flowers, you said."

"Lordy, yes. I can see Mathilde now, bringing in an apron full and dumping them in the sink where I was trying to peel the potatoes. Black-eyed Susans were her favorites. Uncle Jonathan said it was because they matched her eyes. Mathilde had the blackest eyes you'd ever want to see, and when she smiled it was as if little sunbeams twinkled out of them. Lord bless her, she was a lovely woman."

"Her eyes are still beautiful," Holly agreed. "I noticed them as I was giving her lunch. But I'd hardly call them black."

Annie sighed. "My poor old head, I keep forgetting. She's changed, dearie, changed so nobody would know her. It's awful, seeing a fine-looking woman go like that. Dearie, you weren't thinking of making a nice cup of tea any time soon?"

"Right this minute."

Delighted that Annie was at last showing some interest in taking nourishment, Holly limped downstairs and filled the old brown Betty. Annie would have had it stewing on the back of the stove since breakfast. Tomorrow morning, or maybe the day after, she'd be down here slopping around in her ratty blue cardigan, letting the porridge spatter all over the stove.

How could you get to love somebody so much on such short acquaintance?

Annie drank her tea without coaxing, asked for the chamber pot, then murmured that she thought she'd enjoy a little nap. That was all right. Holly took the cup back to the kitchen and started preparing braised beef with potatoes, carrots, onions, and the turnip Bert would surely yell for if she left it out. She'd make enough to warm over for tomorrow night's supper, and save herself some bother.

When she went out to dump the vegetable parings in the garbage pit down behind the stone wall, she noticed a black-eyed Susan she'd neglected to pick. How could that center ever have matched Mrs. Parlett's eyes? People's eye color did often tend to fade as they got older, but what fantastic quirk of nature had turned Mathilde's from almost black to that divine shade of hazel?

Maybe Dr. Walker would be able to explain it when she went back to have her leg checked. It was bothering her a lot, no doubt from too much climbing up and down stairs. He'd tell her to go to bed and stay there, but how could she? As a slight concession to her infirmity, she stretched out on the kitchen cot with a mildewed novel Annie must have been reading. She could keep an eye on the cooking while she relaxed. This wasn't such a bad place to be, with the stove glowing red through the slits in the damper and good smells puffing out of the stewpot as its lid bumped gently up and down.

Holly turned the page. Harold was clasping Vivienne to his manly bosom, his burning cheek resting tenderly on her perfumed cloud of golden tresses. She wouldn't mind being clasped to a manly bosom herself, if it was the right bosom. Now Harold was raising a clenched fist and vowing to avenge his adored Vivienne if it took his last and ultimate breath. There was a chap who didn't mind getting involved. What slush! She laid the book down and closed her eyes.

Then she heard Bert's voice. "Huh! Anybody could walk in here and carry you off."

"They'd darn soon bring me back," Holly answered. "I wasn't asleep, just resting my eyes."

"I've used that one a few times myself. How's Annie?"

"Better. I poured an eggnog into her at noon and a while back she asked for a cup of tea. Don't you think that's a good sign?"

"Is it a good sign if a feller asks for a snort of rum?"

"That depends on whether he's filled the woodbox. I'm cooking you a potroast to make up for all those beans."

"Heck, that reminds me, I brung a little ice cream. Annie always was kind o' partial to strawberry."

"Bert, that's sweet. Give it to me before it melts. I'll put it in the fridge."

He handed over the brown-paper bag sheepishly, as if afraid she might think he was a sissy. "I got some more stuff, too. Claudine phoned up an' told Miz Howe to have me stop by for somethin' you wanted."

"Good, it's time she learned there are other kinds of soup than chicken. What's this weeny little box?"

"That's for you. The drugstore sent it. Claudine says she found it in her mailbox with a note."

Holly read the typewritten message. "Miss Howe forgot part of her prescription. The dose is one at bedtime and one in the morning."

"Oh. Maybe that's why my leg still hurts. Thanks, Bert. I must call Claudine and thank her, too. I'm afraid I wasn't very polite about the soup."

"Well, do it after we eat. Cripes, I could chew on a stove lid. That sister-in-law o' yours wouldn't part with a crumb if a man was starvin' to death on 'er doorstep."

"All right, go get the wood. I'll have supper on the table in three shakes of a lamb's tail." That was what she'd heard Annie say. "You may have your rum for dessert when I go up to feed

my patients. Oh, all right." Holly laughed at his woebegone
face and got down the bottle.

"Ah, that's the stuff!" Bert gulped his tot, wiped a hand
across his grizzled whiskers, and ambled cheerfully off to the
woodpile. When he came back, Holly had the meat and vegetables all dished up. He sat down and swooped upon the food
like a starving wolverine.

"By the Lord Harry, if you was thirty years older, I'd marry
you. Ain't nothin' kills an old man faster'n a young wife. I seen
that Cawne feller givin' you the eye. Dern fool. He's fifty if he's
a day."

"I'd have said forty," Holly protested.

"That's 'cause you don't know no better. He don't fool me
none with his pansy clothes an' that snazzy limousine he
drives."

"It's not a limousine, it's a sports car."

"Some sport he is. Where in tarnation does he get the money
for a buggy like that, is what I'd like to know. Schoolteachers
don't make nothin' to speak of."

"He's not exactly a schoolteacher, Bert. He's a professor, a
traveling lecturer, and a well-known author."

"What did he ever write?"

"Why, I don't know. I'll phone down to the library and find
out, if it will make you feel any better."

"Save your breath. I don't give a hoot. Any more turnips in
the pot?"

"Plenty. Give me your plate, if you can let go of it long
enough." Holly got up and ladled him out another generous
helping.

Bert sent the second load the way of the first. "There, by
cripes. I ain't et, I've dined." He belched contentedly and
picked his teeth with his thumbnail, happy as a gambler with
two aces up his sleeve.

"Want some of your ice cream for dessert?" Holly asked him.

"That's for Annie. Why don't you go on up and give it to
her?"

"Leaving the rum handy?"

"Since you're kind enough to suggest it." Bert poured himself another generous slug, took off his boots with much grunting and puffing, settled himself in the rocking chair, stuck his feet in the oven, and cuddled the thick glass tumbler in both gnarled hands. Holly could stay upstairs with her patients as long as she liked. Bert wasn't going to miss her.

Holly ladled out a cupful of rich broth from the stewpot for Mrs. Parlett. Then she prepared a sort of hearty soup for Annie by dicing bits of meat and vegetables and moistening them with broth. It must be positively seething with vitamins, and Annie was hungry for it.

"That's real tasty, dearie. I declare, I don't know when food's tasted so good to me."

"That's because you're getting better. Finish it up. Your boyfriend brought you a special treat."

"Who?"

"Bert, of course. He says you like strawberry ice cream."

"So I do, but I never thought he'd remember." Tears filled the old housekeeper's eyes as she spooned the pink sweetness in tiny bites to make it last longer. "Land's sakes," she murmured over and over, "to think he'd remember."

Chapter 24

"Your ice cream made a big hit," Holly remarked as she took the empty tray back into the kitchen.

Bert didn't hear. He was dead to the world, lolling back in the rocking chair with the half-full tumbler clutched to his chest. Holly took the drink away and set it on the table, wrinkling her nose at the smell. Whatever had possessed Claudine to send such rotgut?

Maybe this was what Claude Parlett used to drink. If so, no wonder he'd landed down among the lobsters. Holly was standing with the bottle in her hand wondering if she ought to pour the rest of it down the sink when Sam Neill tapped on the window.

"Taking to drink, eh?"

"Thinking about it." Holly set the bottle back on the table. "If you've come for your uncle, forget it. He's out like a light."

"That doesn't surprise me any. Feel like coming for a walk?"

"No, but I'll sit out in the yard and talk for a while, if you like."

"That'll do. I'm here on serious business."

She was too tired to play games tonight. "Were you here on serious business Saturday around midnight, by any chance?"

To her surprise, he grinned. "Oh, you saw me, did you?"

"You almost stepped on me. I was curled up beside the wall pretending to be a rock."

"Why didn't you say something?"

"In the first place, I wasn't sure it was you. In the second, I didn't know why you'd come prowling in the dead of night. I still don't," she added flatly.

"I know, that's what I want to talk to you about. After I left you the other night, I got to thinking about Ellis and his lobster pot. Here, sit down on the wall, I promise not to step on you."

Neill sat beside her, close enough so that she could feel the warmth of his body. "I'm not saying Ellis and I were ever what you'd call buddies, but I've known him all his life, pretty much. It was rough on him and Claudine, with that loud-mouthed drunk of a father and having their mother go the way she did."

"How did she go?" Holly asked.

"Nobody knows for sure. Alice Parlett was always a strange sort of woman. She snubbed everybody in the village, didn't want her kids to play with the rest because they were Parletts even though they didn't have a whole pair of shoes among 'em. I expect Annie's told you some of the family history."

"Yes she has. Alice died quite young, didn't she?"

"She seemed old to me, but you know how kids are about anybody over eighteen. Anyway, Alice was always a touchy woman, but after Claude died she became plain impossible. She'd get into fights at the store, claiming somebody else had grabbed what she was reaching for, silly things like that. Then she took to staying in the house with the blinds down, never going out at all. My mother went to see if she was sick, finally, but she didn't get in. Claudine said her mother was resting and couldn't be disturbed. Nobody was allowed but the doctor. Then one day a hearse from Moncton hauled up in front of the door. All Claudine would say was that her mother had died of pneumonia."

"But if Alice was that sick, why didn't they take her to a hospital?"

"Don't ask me. Mum's theory is that Alice had cancer of the face and wouldn't let anybody see her because she was too horribly disfigured. That could be why the casket wasn't opened at the funeral."

"Do you believe that?"

Neill shrugged. "It's as good a reason as any, and more charitable than some."

"But wouldn't Dr. Walker say what really happened?"

"Uncle Ben doesn't talk about his patients, not even to Mum. Anyway, he didn't know. He was in Europe at the time. A young chap just out of medical school filled in for him. Poor guy, we read in the papers that he'd been killed in a private plane crash not long after he left here."

"Then that means there's nobody left alive but Claudine who knows."

"I suppose Ellis must. Look, I don't know how we got off on this tangent about Alice Parlett. It was Ellis I started to tell you about." Sam rubbed a knuckle over the bridge of his nose, a gesture of old Bert's that Holly was tickled to see. "You may have got the notion Ellis is the village idiot, but he's not. Ellis's problem is that he's an efficiency expert."

"What's wrong with that?"

"The way he interprets efficiency. At school, Ellis spent so much time trying to figure out the easiest way of doing his work that he never managed to finish anything. Once the teacher made him stay after school to write 'I must finish what I start' five hundred times on the blackboard. Ellis spent about half an hour trying to strap ten pieces of chalk between two rulers so he could write ten sentences at once, then found he couldn't write with the darn thing at all. That's been the story of his life, pretty much."

"But Sam, if Ellis is always trying to save work—"

"That's what I'm driving at. Why row a heavy old chest of drawers all the way to Parlett's Point when he could get the veneer off just as easily by tossing it into the pond behind his own house? Folks are so used to Ellis's brainstorms that they've taken this lobster pot business as just one more for the list, but when I got to thinking, it didn't fit in."

"So you rowed out later that same night and hauled up the chest to find out what he'd put in the drawers besides rocks."

"Not much gets by you, eh?"

"It's just that my leg was hurting and I couldn't sleep. My room looks out over the bay. So what did you find?"

"I'm not quite sure. It seemed to be a lot of doodads like candlesticks and figurines. He had them all carefully wrapped in plastic and packed in nylon bags such as skin divers use. I didn't know what to think. It's awfully easy to tag a kid a crook just because his old man was always getting jugged for one thing or another."

"So you drove all the way back here from Saint John Sunday night to do a big brother act?"

"No," Sam growled, "I came because I was worried about you, if you want to know. The only two places I could think of where Ellis might find anything worth hiding like that were his sister's shop and Cliff House. I knew he'd never have the guts to rob Claudine, so I figured the stuff must have come from here."

"The possibility never crossed your mind that he and she might be in it together?"

"Never. Claudine wouldn't do a thing like that."

"Forgive me if I've offended you," Holly said spitefully.

"What's that supposed to mean?"

"I merely wished to congratulate you on your taste. Claudine's a handsome woman even if she does have the personality of a barracuda."

Sam stared at Holly, then the corners of his mouth began to lift. "So that's what's been eating you."

"Not at all. It's no concern of mine if you go rolling in the poison ivy with every woman from here to Vancouver."

"For your information," Sam yelled, "Claudine Parlett used to be my baby-sitter. How could I get romantic about somebody who used to twist her hands into the neck of my pajamas and march me off to bed half-choked when I wanted to stay up and watch television? Speaking of baby-sitters, however, I understand you've acquired one of your own."

"That's a detestable thing to say! Just because an agreeable, cultured gentleman shows a little common courtesy—"

"An agreeable, cultured gentleman," he mimicked in a mincing squeal. "I thought you had brains enough not to fall for a middle-aged baloney artist."

"And I thought we were discussing your baby-sitter. Why don't you believe Claudine and Ellis are working a racket together?"

"Because Claudine wouldn't be fool enough to trust Ellis any farther than she could throw him, that's why. She knows he'd go off on some tangent or other and gum up the works. I thought if I kept watch here I might get a clue to what he's trying to pull."

"You got one last night. Didn't you notice the odd way Ellis's buoy started jerking up and down all of a sudden, and then stopped?"

"Yes, but that must have been an underwater eddy."

"What do you want to bet this particular Underwater Eddie was wearing a frogman's suit?"

"Scuba diving at night off Parlett's Point? Holy cats, I never thought of that. But why not, if he had somebody at the other end of a lifeline ready to haul him out if he got into trouble? The tide was right and he had the buoy to guide him. Who could it be? I can't think of anyone around here who'd be apt to try it."

"I was thinking of someone off a yacht."

"You might have something there. If his contact were anybody local, they wouldn't have to go through all that business, just meet out on a back road and transfer the loot. Using the dresser would allow for flexibility in some outsider's making the pickup. The stuff could stay in the drawer a week or more if necessary. All right, I'm willing to buy your diver. Where'd he go?"

"I pictured a small boat hidden under the cliff," said Holly.

"Wouldn't it be feasible to keep close to shore and avoid being seen until you were ready to make a dash for the yacht?"

"Sure. It would be a lot safer, too. You'd have to be a mighty strong swimmer to buck that current for any distance with a bunch of loaded nets tied to your belt."

Holly winced. Back in Westchester, Fan's swimming awards from camp and college had been whimsically displayed all over the downstairs powder room. Had Sam seen them at Howe Hill? To her surprise, tears began rolling down her cheeks. "Oh Sam," she whispered, "I'm so tired."

"Sure you are."

Now it was the way it ought to be. His arms were tight around her, her face buried in warm, man-smelling flannel. Holly stayed where she was until something had to be done about her sniffles. Had she been Vivienne of the novel, her Harold doubtless would have produced an impeccable square of white linen, but she and Sam hadn't so much as a second-hand Kleenex between them. Regretfully, she wriggled out of his embrace.

"I've got to blow my nose. Don't go away."

"What kind of fool do you think I am? Hurry back."

Holly ran into the kitchen, grabbed a clean cup towel, and mopped her eyes and nose. Through the window she could see Sam Neill watching the door for her to come out, with a look on his craggy face she wanted to remember forever.

She stood hugging the moment to herself until a horrendous crash broke the spell. Bert had fallen out of the rocking chair.

Chapter 25

Bert didn't wake up. That was the incredible part. He lay in a huddle on the grimy braided rug, snoring as though nothing had happened. Holly knelt and shook him by the shoulders. "Bert! Bert, get up. You can't lie there."

He didn't budge. She got a tumbler of water and sprinkled some on his nose. Not an eyelash quivered, not even when she panicked and dashed the whole glassful straight in his face. She was thumping frantically at his chest when Sam called, "What's taking you so long?"

"It's Bert," she gasped. "He's fallen and I can't get him up. You'd better come in here."

He barged through the door. "What's the old soak been drinking?"

"Some rum Claudine sent up. It's dreadful stuff."

"Where's the bottle?"

"Right here." She handed it to him. He pulled out the cork and took a whiff.

"Did you have any of this?"

"No, none. I don't drink. Annie had some Saturday night and she's been deathly sick in bed ever since."

Sam took a few drops on his finger and touched them to his tongue, then spat into the sink. "No wonder. Tastes to me like chloral hydrate."

"Knockout drops? Sam, I don't believe it!"

"Why not? He's knocked out, isn't he?" Sam shoved the stopper back into the bottle. "I'm going to take this down to

Uncle Ben for analysis. If he finds what I think he will, I guess we call in the police."

"Oh, Sam, that sounds so—drastic."

"Holly, this is a drastic situation. That rum wasn't meant just for Bert, was it?"

"I shouldn't think so. Claudine wouldn't know I never touch liquor, and she surely must know Annie likes her little nip. I can't see Claudine giving Annie anything that would hurt her, though."

"Maybe Claudine didn't know what she was sending," said Sam. "Ellis could have loaded the bottle when she wasn't looking."

"But he'd have to break the seal."

"So what? If Annie should happen to notice, she'd naturally assume Bert had helped himself to a drink on the way out from town."

Holly thought that one over, then shook her head. "I know what I'd do. I'd find out what brand it was and get another bottle of the same kind. Then I'd take the seal off carefully, put in the chloral hydrate, and stick the seal back on. When I got a chance, I'd switch bottles. It would be easy enough to do in the shop while the groceries are sitting there waiting to be collected. People are always wandering in and out, I expect, and Claudine can't be watching them every minute."

"All right, that sounds plausible. Who'd you suggest?"

"Earl Stoodley, for one. He does want Mrs. Parlett to die, Sam. He practically told me so on Sunday. You can ask Geoffrey Cawne. He heard it all, including what I said when I blew my stack and told Earl off. Suppose Annie and I had both drunk it and got sick? How long do you think Mrs. Parlett would last without anybody to wait on her? You can't imagine how frail she is. And furthermore, suppose your uncle does find chloral hydrate in the bottle? Who's going to believe Claudine didn't put it there? Then Earl can have her disqualified or impeached or whatever they do, and he'll be the only trustee. You can imagine what will happen then."

"I sure can. Earl's got a fixed idea this museum scheme is going to make him the great man of Jugtown. These loonies with a righteous cause do tend to think the end justifies the means."

He rubbed his knuckles against his nose again. "But if Earl's so fired up to get his museum started, why's he pinching the exhibits? That's assuming the doped rum has anything to do with the stuff in Ellis's dresser."

"Maybe he's raising some quick capital to fix the place up."

"I can't imagine why. There'll be money coming with the estate, and Earl's a well-to-do man in his own right, though you'd never think so to look at him. His father left him a lot of mining stock and he lives on the dividends. That's how he has time to take on these nonpaying jobs so he can throw his weight around."

"Then maybe there isn't any connection between the thefts and the doping. If Earl's so itchy to get started on his project—"

"I can't buy that, Holly. The simplest explanation's most apt to be the right one. I'd say Ellis Parlett and whoever's working with him just wanted to make sure everybody at Cliff House got a good night's sleep so they wouldn't be interrupted at an awkward moment. Your being here creates a new problem for them, don't forget. When Annie was alone with Mrs. Parlett, they didn't have to worry so much. She'd hear what she thought was old Jonathan's ghost prowling around, lock herself in her room, and say her prayers. They must realize it's going to take more than a phony ghost to keep you quiet."

Holly sighed. "I hate to admit it, but you're probably right. And you must be right about Claudine's not knowing what Ellis is up to as well because if she did, she wouldn't have hired me. We'd better get Bert up on the couch."

"Leave him where he is. Serve the old soak right."

"Sam, we can't do that! This floor is terribly drafty. He'd catch pneumonia for sure."

"Small loss if he did." Nevertheless, Sam bent and slid his

arms under his uncle's shoulders. "Take his ankles, will you? One-two-three, heave!"

They lifted Bert to the cot, tucked the afghan around him, and slid a cushion under his head. "Do you think he'll be warm enough?" Holly fussed.

"He's got plenty of anti-freeze aboard." Sam gave his aged relative an affectionate belt on the clavicle. "Throw an old horse blanket or something on top if it'll make you feel better. I suppose the cold does get into the bones, at his age. He's really my great-uncle, though he hates to admit it. Sort of like the old cuss, don't you?"

"I think he's the most enchanting man I've ever met."

"That so?" He tilted her chin so her mouth would be easier to get at. "Who's the second most?"

"Stop it! He'll wake up and be jealous."

"The hell with him."

After a while, Sam let her come up for air. "You going to be my girl?" he mumbled into her hair.

"I thought I already was." Holly took a tighter fistful of his shirt. "Oh, Sam, I wish you never had to let me go."

"I don't."

"Yes you do. I have to put Annie on the pot."

"Let her pee the bed."

"She'd rather die. Come on, be good."

Unwillingly he released his grip. "All right, go tend your babies. I'm going to have a look around outside."

"Will you come back before you leave?"

"Who says I'm leaving?"

"Sam, I can't let you upstairs, and Bert's already grabbed the cot. You've got to get a decent night's sleep, and there's no way you'd get it here."

"Yes, Mother." He tweaked her ponytail. "I suppose I should try to catch Uncle Ben about that rum before he goes to bed. Besides, I promised Roger I'd be on deck early tomorrow to make up for the time I've lost, and this is no time to start a family feud. I guess I'd better slide along. Lock the door after me and don't open it to anybody."

Chapter 26

One last, crushing squeeze and Sam was gone, leaving Holly feeling exposed, chilly, and dreadfully vulnerable. She secured the locks, listened to Bert's gurgling snores long enough to make sure he was safe to be left alone, then went upstairs.

She had a vague recollection that she'd meant to hang around downstairs and find out whether anybody tried to get in the windows she'd screwed shut, but she couldn't. Not tonight. Annie was going to need nursing again tomorrow and maybe for some time to come. She couldn't get through another day of trays and sheets and rubbing backs without a decent night's sleep.

That reminded her, she had two pills to take, not one. It was rather odd, that second half of the prescription turning up in Claudine's mailbox. Very odd indeed, considering the chloral hydrate in the rum. She'd better skip the pill until she'd talked with Dr. Walker and made darn sure he was, in fact, the one who'd sent it.

Holly put on a fresh nightgown and went to change Mrs. Parlett's diaper, hoping she herself would never come down to having some stranger powdering her withered buttocks so she wouldn't develop bed sores. At least old Mathilde still had somebody to do it, in spite of Earl Stoodley. Holly brought fresh water and propped up the lolling head. There'd been water in the carafe on the night stand, but she didn't dare trust anything that had been sitting around Cliff House, not now.

"Come on, take a sip for Holly."

The lids fluttered, showing a glimpse of those incredible

eyes. Was Mathilde signaling that she understood? Anyway, she was drinking. After a moment, Holly took the glass away.

"That's enough for now. I don't want you having to sleep in a puddle."

She surprised herself by bending and kissing Mathilde's cheek. "Sleep tight. I'm going to see if Annie's okay."

Holly was in the bathroom getting warm water and a washcloth for Annie when the phone rang. She limped downstairs and snatched up the receiver, expecting to hear Sam's voice. To her surprise, it was Claudine.

"Holly, I know it's late to phone, but is everything all right?"

"Why?" Holly asked her. "Should something be wrong?" Such as people passing out from knockout drops, or pills the doctor didn't send?

"It's just that with Annie down sick, and your bad leg—"

"Claudine, I told you about that before you hired me."

"I know, Holly, and I'm not blaming you. Truly I'm not. I expect I made the job sound a lot easier than it is. But you looked so nice, and I was so desperately worried—"

Now was as good a time as any to speak her piece. "Maybe it's none of my business," Holly said, "but I think you're making things unnecessarily hard for yourself and all of us by refusing to enter Cliff House. After all, Mrs. Parlett is old and helpless now."

"Holly, you don't understand." Claudine was sobbing, making no attempt to pretend she wasn't. "I'm not harboring a grudge. I'm past that. I just—can't come."

"Why not?"

"I can't tell you. I don't even know why I'm talking to you. Oh God, what am I going to do?"

Abruptly Claudine's voice changed, became firm and crisp as usual. "You'll have to manage as best you can. I'll check with you in the morning. Good night."

She clicked off. Holly stood there with the receiver in her hand until it started making exasperated noises at her.

"Oh, shut up!" She slammed it back on the hook and slumped into a chair. It was easy enough to guess why Claudine had broken off that strange conversation. Somebody had come in, somebody who mustn't know how upset she was. Ellis was the obvious person, but why should she hide her feelings from her own brother?

Why shouldn't she? Roger was Holly's brother, but would she ever try to share an emotion with him? Claudine was Ellis's big sister, the dominant one. Maybe she hadn't wanted him to know she could cry. But why not? She was human, surely; more human than one would have expected. And if it wasn't Ellis, who was it? Why couldn't Claudine have said something like, "Oh hello, Mary. I'll be right with you," so Holly would understand why she'd had to ring off like that?

Holly thought of phoning Sam and getting him to sneak over and find out who the visitor was. And what if he got caught spying on Claudine? He needed his rest after all that backing and forthing to Saint John, and she didn't need him getting hurt. Anyway, there was only one person other than Ellis who'd be likely to barge in on Claudine at this hour. That would be her fellow trustee, Earl Stoodley.

And that made a lot of sense. Simple, venal common sense. Those mining stocks of Earl's must have stopped paying dividends, so he'd decided to mine Cliff House instead. As trustees, he and Claudine had a clear field. Who else could set up a security system to keep out anybody who might realize genuine antiques were being exchanged for fakes? Who else could make a great fuss about a museum while secretly stalling things along until the house had been milked of everything worth stealing? Who else had a ready-made outlet for the loot?

Claudine's anxiety about keeping her great-aunt alive made sense, too, in an ugly way. She must be worried sick over what could happen when Mrs. Parlett died and Earl ran out of excuses to keep the appraisers away from Cliff House.

Likely it wouldn't have been hard for a wily old fox like Stoodley to rope Claudine in. He'd have known how to harp on

Claude's having been done out of his so-called rights; how to rub salt in the wound of Alice's being disinherited and given such a hard life when money might have even prevented that mysterious terminal illness. He could have talked young Claudine into thinking she was only taking what should have been due to her and Ellis in the first place.

So now all Holly had to do was call in the Mounties and—what? Prove Roger's only customer, Mrs. Brown, was in fact just a front for Earl Stoodley? Expose her brother as a maker of fakes instead of a dedicated master craftsman? Maybe Roger and Fan were in on the thefts and maybe they weren't, but who was going to believe they'd dealt with the alleged Mrs. Brown in sublime innocence and good faith? Who'd accept the fact that Roger's sister had been fool enough to take and keep a job at Cliff House without being a party to the ongoing fraud?

After all, what difference would it make if she kept her mouth shut? The antiques were gone, probably sold and resold until they'd never be traced. The museum would be talked of but never opened, not while Earl Stoodley could keep things snarled up in confusion and red tape. Those pictures he was supposedly so keen on letting Geoffrey Cawne take would somehow never get printed. Roger's handiwork would sit gathering dust at Cliff House while he sat a few miles away at Howe Hill wondering why Mrs. Brown never came back to buy any more of his masterpieces.

Or maybe Earl would skip with Mrs. Brown, whoever she might be, leaving Claudine to sweat it out alone. He might even find another house to burgle in the same leisurely fashion, hiring Roger to turn out his expert copies and stick on his pathetic little brass plaques, persuading himself that he was thereby spreading his own fame.

Keeping quiet wouldn't work. Sooner or later the truth would have to come out. No matter who escaped, the Howes were going to be in the soup. Aside from that, Holly herself couldn't be a party to such a crime. Cliff House was a part of

Canada's heritage. The ripping-off wasn't over, it was still going on and it had to be stopped. Feeling older than Mrs. Parlett, Holly heaved herself out of the chair and went back to bed.

But not to sleep. Her mind wouldn't quiet down. There was something, there had been something for a while now, nagging at the back of consciousness; something she'd learned but hadn't connected up.

And she knew what it was! Holly shot out of bed again, grabbed her bathrobe, and slipped downstairs. She didn't know why she was moving so soundlessly, risking a bad fall by not turning on lights. Annie wouldn't mind being wakened, and it would take more of a hullabaloo than one exhausted assistant nursemaid could make to bring Mrs. Parlett back from Never-Never Land.

Nevertheless she didn't flick on the flashlight she'd brought along until she was inside Jonathan Parlett's library with the door shut and the heavy draperies pulled tight across the windows.

The book ought to be on one of the lower shelves. She was sure she'd noticed it when she was prop-hunting for Geoffrey Cawne. Yes, here it was: a thick volume covered in dark red buckram with gold lettering. Dr. Somebody's Home Medical Guide. She had to thumb through the pages a while before she found the reference she wanted. It wasn't a word many people knew. She wouldn't have, herself, if she hadn't been stuck in that hospital ward for so long next to an LPN with a broken hip who fancied herself as an expert on rare diseases.

So that was that, another simple answer to an impossible question. Holly shut the book and put it back on the shelf as guiltily as if she'd been caught reading someone's secret diary. Then she went to wake Bert.

Chapter 27

"Bert! Bert, wake up." Holly shook and pummeled the hired man until he quit snoring and began to grunt.

"Whassamarr?"

"Get up. I have to talk to you."

"Cripes." He swung his bandy legs over the side of the cot and hunched over, clutching his head. "Who hit me?"

"You've been drugged." She hauled him upright and skated his unwilling feet over the varnished linoleum. "Come on, you need fresh air."

"Quit shovin'. Can't you let a—"

Blam!

The explosion sent them both reeling into the back entryway, which probably saved their lives. The stovepipe shot across the kitchen in a spurt of blazing orange. They'd barely got the door unlocked when the whole kitchen was one mass of flames.

"Christ A'mighty!"

Bert was either swearing or praying. It seemed impossible they could be safe out here in the yard, sucking in shuddering lungfuls of smoky, cinder-laden, but still breathable air. Bert reacted the faster, in spite of being still half doped.

"We got to get help!"

He made a dash for the truck, but Holly grabbed at his sleeve.

"Wait, Bert. Annie's in there. Come on!"

Cursing and yelling, he ran after her, around to the front of the house where they might still have some hope of getting in.

Holly wrapped a fold of her bathrobe around her fist and smashed out one of the windows she'd been so proud of bolting shut. Somehow, they got through without tearing themselves to pieces.

Luckily Holly'd hung on to her flashlight. They managed to see their way to Annie's room even though smoke was already beginning to filter through the heavy oak door that shut off the staircase from the back of the house. Annie, incredibly, was sleeping like a baby.

"Come on, you old fool." With surprising tenderness, Bert wrapped his long-time friend in a blanket and tried to pick her up, but he was still too shaky from the knockout drops. Quickly, Holly slid her hands under Annie's armpits.

"Take her feet, Bert."

Together they bundled the by now semiconscious and totally panic-stricken housekeeper out of the room and down the stairs, coughing as the smoke got into their lungs, needing to rub the smart from their eyes but not able to spare a hand to do it. Once Bert slipped, once Holly turned her ankle and almost sent the three of them head first down the long staircase. By the time they'd managed to wrestle the front door open and get Annie out on the lawn, she was unconscious again.

"She don't look so good."

Bert was right. Even the lurid glare of the flames now threatening the roof was putting no color into Annie's face. Her breath was coming in strange, frightening gasps.

"She's having a fit or something," said Holly. "We've got to get her to the doctor, if your truck hasn't caught fire yet. Give me your car keys, quick."

"Hell, this is man's work." Bert bowlegged it to the rear drive where he'd left the ancient pickup while Holly prayed the gas tank wouldn't blow up in his face. Somehow, though, he threaded his way through that flaming No-Man's Land and pulled up beside the prostrate Annie.

Together, they heaved her aboard. Then Bert hopped back into the driver's seat.

"Climb in here, fast!"

Holly had one foot in the cab when she remembered. "You go. I'll wait for the firemen. Hurry!"

Bert opened his mouth to argue, but a shrub close to his right front wheel caught a flying ember and he wasted no more time. He was down the drive and Holly was alone with the inferno that had been Cliff House and the horrifying knowledge that Mrs. Parlett was still upstairs.

As she rushed back through the front door, she knew she was being insane. Even if the frail creature hadn't already suffocated; even if Holly did somehow manage to get her out before they both burned to death, she most likely wouldn't survive being dragged out into the chilly night.

"She's going to die soon anyway," Holly kept telling herself as she panted up the stairs. Still she went on, praying the heavy doors would hold a few seconds longer.

The air in the stairwell was almost unbreathable now, but in the huge master bedroom at the front, it was less intolerable. She rushed in, slammed the door, flung up the window that faced out on that absurd porch roof with its fancy iron railing. She spent precious moments padding the wasted body with the velvet comforter. That window was their only hope now. How she'd manage to get Mrs. Parlett down over the porch roof without killing them both, God only knew; but it was either try or fry.

She couldn't lift the inert body, light as it was, so she dragged it across the floor, got Mrs. Parlett up over the windowsill somehow, and eased her down to the roof. For the first time, perhaps, in its existence, that railing would serve a useful purpose, holding its owner from plunging to the ground before Holly could rig a sling.

Those sheets people in books were always ripping up at times like this couldn't have been these superb, fine-woven linen affairs with heavy tatted edges that wouldn't come loose no matter how frantically one tugged. Holly had to attack the fabric with nail-file, buttonhook, lovely ivory-handled implements from the carved rosewood dressing table that would soon be ashes.

She got the ripping started at last, tore off wide strips, knotted them together as tight as she could. The varnish on the door was rising in huge blisters, the smoke getting thicker, the roaring of the flames incredibly loud. She got out on the roof a split second before the door blew in, slammed the window behind her to gain perhaps another second's grace, and fumbled her makeshift rope around the velvet-covered bundle that lay so very still against the railing. Maybe Mrs. Parlett was already dead. Maybe she would be, too, soon. No matter. They'd go on.

She tied the other end of her sheet rope around that blessed railing, heaved the body over the edge of the roof, and began to lower it slowly, carefully even though she could feel the heat through the glass at her back. The window would explode, just as that floodlight had done. She'd be full of flying glass again. Why didn't the fire truck come?

For an instant, Holly thought she saw somebody out across the drive, and screamed, "Help me!" But it must have been only a trick of the flickering flames and shadows, because nobody came.

That was all right. Mrs. Parlett was safe on the ground and she herself was sliding down, holding to the sturdy linen strip, wrapping her scarred legs around one of the blistering porch pillars; not minding the heat or the smoke or even the bits of flaming debris.

Now she was running, dragging the once-beautiful velvet comforter behind her, grateful that the grass was dry and slick. It was like pulling a child on a sled. Only there should be wonderful, cold snow under her feet and none of these sudden bursts of flame she had to keep darting around.

"Not that way!" Incredibly, someone was running beside her, shouting in her ear, steering her away from the course she'd been blindly following. "Head for the water. Never mind trying to save whatever you've got there. Leave it and run!"

"I can't," Holly gasped. "It's Mrs. Parlett. Help me!"

"Oh, God. Trust you to complicate matters."

Only one person could speak in such a tone of well-bred exasperation at a time like this.

"Geoffrey! How did you get here?"

"I saw the flames and thought I'd better find out where they were coming from. My house sits rather high, you know. How did it start?"

"The kitchen stove blew up." Suddenly Holly knew why. "Somebody dropped a bucket of gasoline down the chimney."

"From a helicopter? Holly, you're hallucinating."

"I am not! I smelled it. I know it was gasoline. I saw a Molotov cocktail tossed into a storefront on Broadway once. The explosion was exactly the same, only this was much worse."

"Very well if you say so. Come on, we've got to get out of here."

Paying no attention to the human bundle she'd risked her life for, he grabbed Holly's arm and tried to hustle her along.

"Mrs. Parlett," Holly screamed. "We can't—"

"To hell with her. Let her stay."

"Geoffrey, no!"

That was another voice. Out of the smoke and the sparks Claudine Parlett ran toward them, shrieking. "Pick her up, quick!"

"Why should I?" asked the professor coolly.

"Because that's not Mathilde, you fool," snapped Holly. "It's Claudine's mother. If you're too scared to help us, get out of the way."

Between them, the two women stooped to lift the bundle. Angrily, Cawne brushed them aside and took Alice Parlett into his arms.

"All right, if you must be totally irrational. Come along. This way."

"But why not down the drive?" Holly protested. "People will be coming."

"And we'll all be dead by the time they get here. Toward

the bay, for God's sake, and stop arguing. Claudine, you've got to help me carry this thing. It weighs a ton."

"Stop calling her 'it,'" Holly raged. "She's more human than you are."

"Thank you." Cawne thrust the velvet-covered burden at her and turned his back.

Claudine snatched to keep her mother from dropping to the ground. Together, she and Holly scrabbled Alice Parlett down over the bank, Geoffrey herding them every step of the way but not lifting a hand to assist. When they reached the bush from behind which she and Sam had watched Ellis set his trap, Holly panted, "This is far enough."

"Until the grass catches fire," said Cawne. "The sensible thing is for you two to keep going down to the ledge. I'll make a dash for my car and come to pick you up."

"You won't have time," Claudine protested. "The tide's on the turn. The ledge will be covered in a few minutes. Look at the bay."

In the reflections now cast high and wide by the leaping flames, they could see an eerie shiver on the surface of the water. Fundy's inexorable flood was about to begin. They might as well be burned as drowned.

"We'll stay here," said Holly. "We're safe enough. The wind's blowing off the water. The grass fire will go the other way."

"And the fire truck will be here any minute," said Claudine. "They were ringing the alarm bell when I left my house."

"Why were you coming here?" Holly asked her point-blank. "Did you know Cliff House was going to be fire-bombed?"

"Oh my God! Is that what happened? No, I didn't know. Holly, you've got to believe me. I'd never have hurt you. I—it was those pills. I was afraid—"

"Shut up," snapped Cawne. "Get down on that ledge, both of you."

Claudine stared at the gun he was poking straight at her face. "Geoffrey, you're mad! I don't believe this."

"You'd better believe it, my dear. You deceived me about your mother, and you'd have betrayed me over those pills. I could never have trusted you again. Goodbye, Claudine. At the risk of sounding trite, I must say I'm sorry it had to end this way."

Claudine stayed frozen. Monstrously, Cawne reached out one foot and set Alice Parlett rolling toward the bay. At that, Claudine turned and ran after her mother, but Holly held her ground.

"You—you—there are no words for you. What was in those pills you sent me? The same stuff that almost killed Annie?"

"Let's just say that if they'd been taken as directed, we'd both have been spared a certain amount of unpleasantness. Damn you, why didn't you take them? Why didn't you take them?"

Cawne started shaking her, screaming like a brat in a tantrum. "It's your fault. I was doing fine until you spoiled everything by finding out about those tables. You deserve to die!"

Step by step he was forcing her backward, maneuvering for a chance to hook her feet from under her and send her hurtling toward the ledge. Holly tried to fight, but her strength was gone. All she had left was her voice, and not much of that.

"Sam! Sam!"

What was the use? Sam was asleep in Jugtown, four miles away. He couldn't hear that feeble croak. Nobody could. Still she called. "Sam! Help me, Sam!"

Something tall and lean came leaping down the hill. Sam's was no expert blow, but it did the job. Cawne sprawled among the hummocks. Holly grabbed for his gun. Sam grabbed for Holly.

"What's he done to you?"

"Tried to kill me. Oh, Sam, how did you find me?"

"Darned if I know. I just came." He rubbed his face in her hair. "You smell like a finnan haddie."

"You've still got your pajamas on."

"So I have." Sam looked down at slightly less than six feet of striped cotton. "That's odd. I don't even remember getting out of bed. No you don't," he roared as Cawne started to crawl away. "Lie still or I'll stomp a hole through you."

Holly started to giggle hysterically. "You can't, you idiot. You're in your bare feet."

"Then I'll claw him to death with my toenails. Here, give me that gun of his before you shoot somebody. Not that it would be such a bad idea," Sam added as he took thoughtful aim.

"See here, Neill," Geoffrey began to bluster, "this is all a stupid misunderstanding. I can explain—"

"Don't bother. Frankly, Cawne, I always did find you a bit of a bore. What am I going to do with this skunk, Holly? If I tie him up with my pajama cord, my pants will fall down."

"Keep him covered. I'll get something. Claudine, where are you?"

"Down here by the cliff. Mother's caught on a bush and I don't dare pull her loose for fear I'll lose my balance and let her fall."

"Hang on, I'm coming."

"What's all this?" Sam demanded, but Holly didn't wait to explain. Claudine was indeed in a precarious position, crouched too close to the edge, clutching at what was left of the comforter with her mother still tied inside. Holly lay down on the ground and stretched out her arms.

"Take my hand and work yourself back to firm ground, keeping hold of the sheet. Lie down the way I'm doing. Then we can both wiggle forward and get a grip on her."

Claudine obeyed. Between them, they managed to pull Mrs. Parlett back to safety.

"If she survives this, it'll be a miracle," Holly panted, "but I did the best I could."

"You've been—what can I say?" Claudine sobbed. "Oh Holly, I never meant to get you into anything like this."

"Of course you didn't. Come on, let's get her up the hill a little farther."

"But Geoffrey will—"

"No he won't. Sam Neill has him on the ground, covered by his own gun. Help me undo these strips of linen. We need them to tie up Geoffrey."

"Let me do it," said Claudine savagely. "I'll tie them around his neck!"

"Take it easy. You're not the first woman who's fallen for a smooth-talking crook."

"I'll be the last, as far as he's concerned."

"Never mind him now. Is your mother still breathing?"

"I—I think so. I can't tell for sure."

Holly left Claudine bent anxiously over Alice Parlett and went back to Sam. Between them, they got Cawne trussed up tight as a mummy.

"He'll do," Sam decided when they'd run out of sheet. "Hey, I hear the fire truck."

"About time."

Then the area was swarming with volunteer firemen. Cliff House was gone, but they could still keep the flames from spreading into the woods. Men stood watching until the tide had completed its incredible inward surge, then rushed down to pump water from the bay.

Holly forgot the tide could have been the death of her. She and Sam got caught up in the confusion, Holly assuring people they'd all got out of Cliff House alive, Sam tugging at hose lines with the other men, making helpful suggestions to which the rugged individualists in the fire brigade paid no attention. It was some time before they remembered their prisoner. When they went to get him, Geoffrey was gone.

Earl Stoodley happened to be nearby, togged out like a fireman but not doing much of anything. Holly grabbed at the sleeve of his rubber coat.

"Did you see Professor Cawne?"

"I sure did," he told her. "He yelled to me for help. He'd been hurt rescuing the old woman from the burning house.

Some fool tried to give him first aid. They got him bandaged so tight he couldn't move. I got out my jackknife and—"

"Cut him loose," Holly finished bitterly. "Come on, Sam. We'd better find Claudine before Geoffrey does."

Chapter 28

Cawne had made no further attempt to silence Claudine. He'd simply made his way through the crowd of firefighters, exchanging an affable word here and there, and driven off in the Jaguar he'd left parked out on the main road.

"That would be Geoffrey," snapped Claudine, pouring coffee for Holly as competently as though she hadn't been up most of the night. "He was always going on about how a man's best weapon is a ready tongue."

Fan had appeared at Parlett's Point somewhere along the line, explaining that Roger couldn't come to find out whether his sister had burned to death because he needed his sleep. She'd offered transportation to Howe Hill, but Holly had elected to go back into Jugtown with Claudine and Sam so that she could be near Annie in case of emergency.

There wasn't going to be one. Annie was in Dr. Walker's spare room suffering from nothing worse than exhaustion and shock, ready to be moved as soon as she had a place to go. Alice Parlett was back in her own girlhood bed above the shop, taking her tea and porridge. Ellis was off somewhere and Bert was still alseep at home, worn out from his ordeal. Holly, Sam, and Claudine were having breakfast in the kitchen behind the antique shop.

"Roger must be having fits because you haven't shown up for work this morning, Sam," Holly remarked.

"Nuts to Roger," said Sam, helping himself to another pancake. "Has it ever occurred to you that my future brother-in-law may have one foot an inch or two around the bend?"

"Often," Holly answered frankly. "I think Fan knows it, too. That could be why she was willing to get him out of New York."

"Well, she came to the right place," Claudine said. "Jugtown's got its share of oddballs, all right." Unconsciously she looked upward, toward Alice Parlett's bedroom.

"It's Alzheimer's disease, isn't it?" Holly asked her gently.

Claudine nodded. "Dr. Walker told me ages ago there wasn't anything we could do except keep her as comfortable as possible till she had to be put away. I wasn't going to let her die in an asylum. I wanted her to have the best, all the things she'd have had if Uncle Jonathan—"

She started to cry. "I begged Dr. Walker never to tell anybody. We both knew what people would say. They'd never heard of anybody her age having such an ailment. They'd claim we were just trying to cover up because Daddy'd given her a—a disease."

Claudine went to pieces then. Holly sat stroking her head, not trying to stop her. Right now, tears were the best medicine. Sam got embarrassed, as men do when women cry, and tried to cope by being brusquely matter-of-fact. "What's Alzheimer's disease?"

"It's a progressive, irreversible, and as far as I know incurable disease that affects the cerebral cortex," Holly told him. "What happens is that the victim becomes forgetful and disoriented, and begins acting strangely. Picking fights for no reason, that sort of thing. As the disease progresses, it affects the parts of the brain that control the organic system. The body is less and less able to function. The victim deteriorates physically and finally dies of what looks like old age, even though he or she may be relatively young. That's why—"

"Why I was able to fool people into thinking Mother was Great-aunt Mathilde," sniffled Claudine. "She's only sixty, but she looks a hundred. Dr. Walker didn't think she'd last long. It's only because Annie took such wonderful care of her. I don't know why. Annie never bothered much about Mother while she was all right."

She sat up and blew her nose on a paper napkin. "Nobody did. Mother was always pretty tough to get along with, I have to admit. But she's still my mother."

"Not many mothers have a daughter like you," said Holly.

"You're right. There aren't that many fools in the world."

"Knock it off," Sam growled. "Listen, Claudine, I know what you went through as a kid. You were brainwashed from the day you were born. Your father was always spouting off about what a great man he'd have been if he hadn't been cheated out of his so-called rights, and your mother backed him up because she couldn't admit she'd been dumb enough to cut her own throat by tying up with a no-good drunk. Maybe that's not very tactful but it's the truth, and you might as well face it."

"I know now, but I had to believe them then. How else could I have stood being the worst-dressed girl in school and having a father who spent half his time in jail?"

"Sam isn't judging you, Claudine," said Holly. "He's just trying to say he understands why you put your mother in Mathilde Parlett's place."

"I didn't murder another old woman to get my mother a bed, if that's what you're thinking. Great-aunt Mathilde died peacefully of old age right after Dr. Walker left, just as he'd said she would. Annie knew we were on the outs, but we were the only Parletts left, so she called us first. She was terribly upset about losing Great-aunt Mathilde and scared stiff about what would happen to her. She was sure Earl Stoodley was going to put her straight out into the snow without a shirt to her back."

"I wouldn't put it past him," Sam grunted. "Go on, Claudine. What did you do?"

"I told her to stay there and keep her mouth shut. Then I got Ellis to help me bundle Mother up and sneak her into that old truck of his, that used to be Daddy's. I'd already gone into the antique business by then, selling off whatever we had of our grandparents' that was worth anything, and picking up the odd piece here and there. We had to live somehow, and I couldn't go out to work on account of Mother. Anyway, we made believe we were setting off on a business trip, or would have if anyone'd asked us, but luckily nobody did. Once we'd got clear of town, Ellis swung around by the back road and made a beeline for Parlett's Point. Annie let us in. We carried Mother up to the bedroom and took Great-aunt Mathilde's body back home with us.

"The next morning I called Dr. Nicholson and told him Mother had died in her sleep. He was brand-new in town, of course, and had never laid eyes on her. He knew from Dr. Walker's records that she had Alzheimer's disease, so he didn't make any trouble about signing the death certificate. He did want to do an autopsy, but I cried and carried on about not wanting poor, dear Mummy cut up, so he backed off. Then we had the best funeral I could afford and buried Great-aunt Mathilde in the family plot, right next to Great-uncle Jonathan. I suppose some people thought we did it for spite, but I didn't care. I'd done what I thought was right. Only it didn't stop there."

Claudine began drawing patterns on the tablecloth with her spoon handle. "You see, what I did gave Ellis the notion that it was all right for him to—well, he started bringing home some pretty good antique pieces and telling me he'd found them at the dump, or out back in those old deserted houses left over from when they had the pottery works. I believed him at first because I wanted to, I suppose. I sold off the pieces to pay our back bills and fix up the shop the way I wanted it. Then I told him he'd better quit finding things because by that time I had a pretty strong hunch where they were coming from. But he did it once more and that time, Geoffrey caught him."

She took a sip of cold coffee and wiped her lips with infinite care. "Geoffrey had just moved to Jugtown. I'd never met him before, though of course I'd heard some of the gossip. He was supposed to be quite famous, though nobody could say exactly why. Anyway, he collared Ellis with a nice cranberry glass compote, and brought him back to the shop. Then we all three sat down for a quiet little talk.

"I thought he was going to lecture Ellis about stealing from Cliff House, and I hoped he'd lay it on good and thick. Instead, he started asking a lot of kind, understanding questions about ourselves, our parents, and our connection with Cliff House."

Claudine shrugged. "I'd only been there the one time we took Mother, and naturally I couldn't admit to that, but I knew enough to keep him interested. Mother used to go on by the hour about the porcelains and the furniture and the twelve nightgowns Great-aunt Mathilde had brought back from Paris while we had nothing to sleep in but one old flannel rag apiece. I guess I gave him quite an earful. Anyway, the next day he was back here looking for things to put in his new house. What he was really looking for, he said, was a pair of wall sconces like the ones I'd described at Cliff House.

"To make a long story short, he politely suggested Ellis should go and steal them for him. He didn't say it in so many words, of course. He's much too clever for that. But I got the message all right. He also dropped a gentle hint that if we didn't get them, he'd have Ellis arrested for stealing the compote."

"That figures," said Holly. "What did you do?"

"Well, I told him no. Then he made believe he was only joking and trying to make me blush because I looked so—I ought to have known he was—but how could I? Nobody'd ever paid me a compliment before."

Claudine spread her hands in a gesture of self-deprecation. "So that was the molasses that caught the fly. After that Geoffrey came in pretty often, and we started having soulful chats about what a rotten deal Ellis and I had got from the Parletts. Of course that was what Mama and Daddy had always claimed. Needless to say, I was happy to hear the same

172 THE TERRIBLE TIDE

thing from a fine, upstanding gentleman like Professor Cawne.

"Then he started making shy, genteel passes at me and by that time I'd have robbed the Royal Bank of Canada if he'd asked me to. But I still wasn't about to involve Ellis, so Geoffrey and I started a little game of our own. We were terribly clever about it. I'd get my hands on some piece that wasn't worth much but resembled one Mother had described. Then Geoffrey would take it out to Cliff House and substitute it for the real thing, which he'd sell to somebody he knew—he'd never tell me who it was—and bring me the money. He said it was his way of making up to me for all I'd been deprived of as a child."

"How touching," said Holly. "Just like Robin Hood."

"As I recall, Robin Hood always managed to keep a healthy slice of the loot for himself," Sam added.

"Roughly eighty percent in my case," Claudine admitted, "though I didn't realize that for quite a while. After I'd learned enough about the antique business to realize how little I was clearing in proportion to what the pieces were really worth, I tried to convince Geoffrey his dear friend was stealing us blind. He was grieved and wounded at my lack of trust. Anyway, it was all clear profit and more money than I'd ever handled before, so I didn't complain too hard. It became easier and easier to believe I was only taking what I was entitled to, especially with Earl Stoodley yammering at me about when was the old woman going to die and let him get his greasy meathooks into the pie? If Earl ever finds out how I tricked him for five whole years, he'll kill me."

"I shouldn't be surprised," Holly agreed. "Earl must be out of his mind, having his dreams of glory go up in smoke. If he only knew the man he helped get away was the one who set the fire!"

"Will you quit harping on Stoodley?" said Sam. "Go on, Claudine. What about Cawne's operation?"

"Where was I? Oh, about Cliff House. Once he started going in there, of course, Geoffrey knew a lot more than I did about what to steal. Instead of my having to wait for a usable piece to come in, he'd give me a list and send me out hunting. I'm not going to pretend I didn't love that. I'd go to Toronto or Montreal, maybe, and sometimes Geoffrey would meet me. We'd have dinner in fancy restaurants, see the ballet or a play, do things I'd only dreamed about. We had to be terribly careful about not acting too friendly in Jugtown, though. That's why I got active in the Women's Circle and—"

"Took long walks in the woods?" Holly put in slyly.

Claudine flushed. "Well, that's over now. At least I've got Mother back, though not for long, I don't suppose. I wonder if Dr. Walker will know who she is?" .

"Uncle Ben's pretty hard to fool," said Sam, "but he'll understand. If you want, I'll tell him the story myself."

"Oh Sam, would you?" Claudine started to cry again. "I didn't think I had a friend in the world, except maybe Annie Blodgett. And what's to become of her now?"

"Don't fret yourself about Annie," said Sam. "She's all set."

"How?"

"You'll know soon enough."

That was a load off Holly's mind, but she still had her own problems to settle. "Claudine, whose idea was it to rope in my brother on the racket?"

"Geoffrey's, of course. I wasn't supposed to have ideas, just carry out orders. After your sister-in-law showed up at the Women's Circle and told us what your brother did, I passed on the information, that's all. Geoffrey checked him out and got excited. You see, we'd had to leave the furniture alone until then. Vases and things were easy enough. Annie's eyesight isn't what it was and I gather that neither is her housekeeping. Besides, she was busy with Mother. So long as we put something more or less the right size and shape in the place she was used to seeing something, she'd never notice the difference. Earl Stoodley was our big problem."

Claudine sighed. "He used to come and blether to me about how many hours he was putting in at Cliff House, planning and measuring and making a general nuisance of himself, no doubt. Earl doesn't know beans about antiques, but he's sharp as a tack in some ways and he was always messing around with the furniture, making little sketches and haranguing me about where the different pieces should go when it came time to set up the museum. That meant we didn't dare take away the originals until we had copies that matched his sketches. And here was Roger Howe, able to turn them out. His being in Jugtown made it harder for us, in a way."

"I can imagine," said Sam. "I mean, you couldn't exactly waltz up to him and say, 'Please make a Sheraton highboy and deliver it to Cliff House,' could you?"

"Hardly. That's why Geoffrey invented Mrs. Brown."

"Who was she?" Holly asked. "Not you, surely?"

"No, Geoffrey himself. He loves disguises. He even fooled me one day when he'd been out to see Roger and walked in here wearing some outlandish New Yorky getup. Green stockings, I remember. How ever did you catch on to his tricks so fast, Holly?"

"How could I miss? The first copy I came across had a stain of my own blood on it."

Holly told them about the Bible box. "After that, it wasn't hard to pick out others, and to find the little holes underneath where Roger's nameplate had been taken off. I'd seen a scrapbook Fan kept with photographs and notes about all Roger's different pieces before I went to Cliff House. Come to think of it, Fan showed the scrapbook to Geoffrey that night he came to dinner at Howe Hill."

"Yes, and he had a fit," said Claudine. "All those notes in his own handwriting, that he thought he'd got back safely! It never occurred to him she might have had them copied."

"So that's why Fan acted so strange about the scrapbook that day Geoffrey drove me back to Howe Hill. I asked to see it and she made a ridiculous excuse not to bring it out. I suppose Geoffrey'd stolen it by then and she didn't dare let Roger know it was missing."

"I'm sure he had. He was cocky enough a day or so later, bragging to me about how he'd had so much fun making you help him take pictures of a piece he was going to get Roger to copy. I warned him you're no fool and I—I'm afraid he did listen to me for once. He said he'd give you a test. I don't know what he meant."

"I do," said Holly. "Sunday morning he came to Cliff House with Earl and set up a group shot using a pair of piecrust tables Roger had made. When I saw what he'd done, I panicked. By then, you see, I'd made up my mind it must be Fan who was working the swindle. I had visions of all us Howes winding up in jail together if the photo ever got published. I thought I was terribly clever about working a razzle-dazzle switch to get the tables out of the shot."

"You were," said Claudine. "That's what bothered Geoffrey. He came in here last night while I was talking on the phone to you. He said you were too bright and would have to go. I asked what he planned to do and he said not to worry, it was already done. Then he left and I remembered about those pills. I grabbed the keys to Ellis's truck and headed for Cliff House as fast as I could. But he beat me."

Claudine buried her face in her hands. "I suppose I'd known for a long time that Geoffrey was only using me. But when you've lived with dreams and illusions all your life, it's hard to face the truth. Oh, God, how I want to be honest! I swear I shan't mind going to jail. At least I'll know where I am."

Chapter 29

"What makes you think we're going to turn you in?" Sam asked her.

Claudine stared at him from under swollen eyelids. "Why shouldn't you? If I hadn't pulled that awful trick with Mother and Great-aunt Mathilde, none of this would have happened. And if it hadn't been for Holly, she and Annie and Mother and Bert Walker would all be dead by now, and it would be my fault."

"Did you know Cawne intended to fire-bomb Cliff House?"

"Of course not! What do you think I am?"

"Did you know what was in that bottle of rum you sent up Saturday?"

"Some kind of mild sedative was what Geoffrey told me. You see, back when Annie was there alone, Geoffrey and his helper would just lock her in her bedroom when they were—working. They moaned around a little, I guess, and made her think it was ghosts. I hated having Annie scared like that, but—"

Claudine swallowed hard. "Anyway, with Holly around, Geoffrey said we'd have to step up our security measures. The sedative was supposed to be an experiment."

"Some experiment!" snorted Neill. "Who put it in the bottle? You?"

"Oh, no. I wouldn't have dared, for fear of poisoning somebody. My part was simply to send the rum on up with the groceries when Bert came. That's why Geoffrey was here in the shop that day, Holly. He had the bottle under his jacket and dropped it in my basket while he was pretending to look at the stock. What a fool I've been!"

She looked ready to burst into tears again. Sam hastily asked her, "Who was the helper? Ellis?"

"Not Ellis. That was part of our bargain from the very beginning. I told Geoffrey I wouldn't go along with him unless we kept Ellis clear out of it. I don't know who helped him. I couldn't go near the place, myself. I'd made that silly remark ages ago that I'd never set foot in Cliff House till we got our rights, and Geoffrey decided I'd better stick with it. Then if the thefts should ever be discovered, nobody would think to suspect me. Besides, it kept Ellis from having any more notions about Cliff House. I kept harping on our having too much pride to go back on our word and that sort of foolishness till he honestly believed we were involved in a big family feud. Ellis is easily led in some ways."

"Then you don't actually know how the furniture was got in and out?" said Holly.

"Only what Geoffrey told me. He'd worked out some kind of arrangement with a warehouse in Saint John. Your sister would deliver the copies there and Geoffrey would go and get them, disguised as a truckman. He always got such a kick out of pretending to be what he wasn't. I sometimes wonder if he's even a college professor."

"I wouldn't bet on it," said Sam. "I tried to read that book of his on the Canadian poets. Most of it was cribbed, and the rest is pure hogwash. As for being a visiting lecturer, all I can say is that makes a great excuse for being someplace else at a convenient time. I sure wish we could find out who's been fencing what he's stolen."

"At least I can ask Fan what warehouse she went to," said Holly. She happened to glance out the window as she spoke and noticed oil spots splashed around the driveway. "Looks as if Ellis's truck is in about the same condition as hers."

"Oh, that old crate," sighed Claudine. "He's forever trying some crazy invention to make it run better, but they never work. It spews oil every time he steps on the gas. He has to keep a bicycle in the back for when it breaks down and he has to pedal back home. Anybody want another cup of tea?"

She was refilling the pot when the truck clattered into the yard. Loaded into its back was a late Victorian dresser, dripping wet and half stripped of its veneer. Sam got up and went to the door.

"Ellis, come in here."

Claudine started to say something, but Holly shushed her. Young Parlett shambled into the kitchen, looking scared.

"Been hauling your traps, eh?" Sam remarked.

Ellis nodded.

"How much was Professor Cawne paying you to help him smuggle furniture in and out of Cliff House?"

"He never paid me a cent!" Ellis turned to his shocked sister. "Honest, Claudine, I'd never have gone against what you made me promise, only he threatened to turn me over to the Mounties. I didn't dare let myself get arrested for fear they'd find out about—" he flushed scarlet and shut his mouth fast.

"It's all right, Ellis," said Holly. "We know about your mother and we're not blaming you for doing what you did. Just tell us what Geoffrey Cawne put you up to."

"He saw me putting a dresser to soak here in the cove once, so he got this bright idea about me doing it out at Parlett's Point instead, buoyed to look like a lobster trap. I wasn't supposed to know why, but I'm not quite so dumb as I look. I hung around till I found out he's got somebody with a thirty-foot yawl who comes up into the bay when the tide's right and sends a skin diver out at night in a dark-blue dinghy to make pickups. I was supposed to leave each piece for a week and not go near it in the meantime. That's what I did. I never pinched anything, not even—"

"Not even after you found out what he was putting in the drawers," Sam finished for him. "Okay, Ellis, I took a peek myself. How did you manage about the furniture?"

"We'd meet out back somewhere and he'd take my truck and drive off in it. He'd be got up in a ratty old flannel shirt and stuff so he looked just like any guy driving a truck. He can change his cap and rub a little dirt on his face and I swear you'd never think it was the same guy."

"So that's why you've been coming home on your bicycle and lying to me about the truck's breaking down," Claudine snapped.

"I had to say something, sis."

"Save it," said Neill. "Go on about the furniture, Ellis."

"Well, the next night I'd have to meet him again out at Parlett's Point. There'd be a big crate in the truck. We'd drive down onto the ledge and rig a hoist up over the face of the cliff. We couldn't take the crate in through the yard, see, for fear Annie would find out and know we weren't ghosts."

He grinned, then caught his sister's eye and sobered in a hurry. Claudine had turned white as a ghost herself.

"Ellis, do you mean to tell me you've been driving that mess of junk down on the ledge? You could have been drowned like a rat in a barrel."

"Aw, what do you take me for? We had to time it right, that was all. I admit I was scared at first, but then it got to be kind of a game."

"So you were playing games the other night," Holly remarked.

"You mean when I locked you in the parlor? I'm sorry about that, but I had to."

"On account of the man going out to the buoy? But I could see that out the window."

"No, that wasn't it. I didn't even know he was coming. I was inventing something, if you want to know."

"Something to dump gasoline down the chimney with?"

Ellis squirmed. "Cawne told me it would only be a smoke bomb. See, having you at Cliff House got him worried. You were too smart. It wouldn't work long for us to just shut you in your room and make funny noises like we did with Annie.

Cawne figured we'd better have some way to create a diversion. That's what he called it. You don't have to glare at me like that, Claudine. All I did was go up through the attic and out the trap door to the roof—"

"Ellis!"

"And fasten a couple of little pulleys to the lightning rods. Then I rigged a fishing line through them and led it over the top of the chimney, and dropped the ends of the line down to the ground. See, all you'd have to do was hitch the smoke bomb to one end of the line and haul on the other end till the bomb was right over the chimney, then slack off and whammo!"

"I guess 'whammo' describes it as well as anything." In spite of himself, Sam began to laugh. "Well, Ellis, at least you've invented one thing that worked."

"I don't see anything funny about trying to make my brother an accomplice to murder," said Claudine bitterly. "If I ever get my hands on Geoffrey Cawne again—"

The shop bell rang. Without waiting for an invitation, Earl Stoodley rushed into the kitchen. "Claudine, I need your name on these insurance papers, quick."

"What for? There's not going to be any Parlett Museum now."

"Never mind the museum. I got a better idea. We clear away the rubble, turn the barn into a recreation hall and the old henhouse into a shower room, put in a few chemical toilets to save the cost of digging a septic tank, and set up a campground. Like Fundy National Park, eh, only smaller. It'll bring in the tourists like—say, you folks heard the news?"

"About what?"

"The professor. Remember I told you he got hurt trying to save Mrs. Parlett? I doctored him up some, but I guess he figured he'd better drive himself down to Dr. Walker. He must have been in a bad way because he was gunning that Jaguar for all she was worth, according to Sergeant MacBeith. They'd got word down at police barracks about the fire and Sarge was on his way up when this gray car came at him hell a-whooping and swerved right into his path. MacBeith swears the driver was trying to force him off the road, but of course we know better. I figure the professor must have passed out from the pain. Anyway, the Jag hit a soft shoulder and skidded down over the cliff. The tide was making then, so there wasn't a thing MacBeith could do but sit and watch."

Stoodley shook his head. "Sarge says it was the awfullest thing he ever had to do, just watching that tide come in over the car. They got tackle down as soon as they could and managed to raise the car, but the professor was dead as a mackerel. Never knew what happened, I don't suppose. It's an awful loss to Jugtown, him and Cliff House both gone in one night, but I'll pull us through in grand style. You wait and see. Any more tea in that pot?"

"Sorry, Earl," said Holly firmly, "we've drunk it all. At least there's one consolation. Mrs. Parlett came through without a scratch and she's resting comfortably upstairs right now. So you'll have to cool it with the tourist camp for a while."

Even Claudine was laughing as the shop door closed on her stricken fellow trustee. Ellis looked from one merry face to another.

"Then you're not going to tell?"

"What is there to tell?" said Holly. "Geoffrey Cawne is dead, Cliff House is burned to the ground, and who'd believe a crazy yarn like this anyway? Right, Sam?"

Neill put his arm around her. "Right. The Parletts have been punished enough already. Anyway, Holly and I have to keep on your sister's good side. We'll be needing my old baby-sitter again one of these days, maybe."

The two young women embraced. The two young men pounded each other on the back. Holly started crying and Sam had to kiss her to make her stop. In the midst of it all, Bert Walker ambled in.

"What are you so all-fired het up about?"

They told him and he nodded. "I knew somethin' was in the

wind soon as Sam bought himself that bottle o' fancy shavin' lotion. Worst-tastin' stuff I ever threw a lip over. Well, there's another good man gone down the drain. Between you an' me an' the bedpost, he might not be the last."

"Bert!" shrieked Holly. "You mean you and Annie—"

"Don't rush me, drat it. I ain't said I'd go so far as to marry 'er yet. But I s'pose I'll have to or Lorraine will chew my ear off. You busted the news to your mother yet, Sam?"

"Haven't had time, but we'll do it today. Speaking of which, Holly, I suppose we'd better mosey on over to Howe Hill. Your brother must be tearing his pretty curls out by now."

"I shouldn't be surprised," sighed Holly. "Wait till he and Fan find out they've lost a Brown and gained a Neill! At least I still have some clothes there, and a bed to sleep in, such as it is."

"Why don't you come to our house?" said Sam. "Mother will be home from the hospital and you two might as well get to know one another. I'm not going to work for Roger any more, but I should be able to steer quite a lot of work his way. Maybe he'd take Ellis on as an apprentice."

"Would you like that, Ellis?" Holly asked. "My brother's not the easiest person to work for, but he is a first-rate craftsman. You might learn something useful if you could stick with him for a while."

"Yes, and you'd be doing honest work for a change," said Claudine. "Go ahead and fix it up if you can, Holly. As for myself, I'm going to sell out the shop here and let Bert and Annie move in downstairs. They can take care of Mother and keep house for Ellis. I'll get a job with one of the big city antique dealers and stay there till I've really learned the business. Then I'll set up my own shop again. But it won't be in Jugtown."

"Oh, I don't know," said Holly, pulling Sam's arm tighter around her. "Jugtown's not such a bad place, once you've gotten to know the people."

ALISA CRAIG was born in New Brunswick, Canada, where THE TERRIBLE TIDE is set. She is the author of three previous novels for the Crime Club, *Murder Goes Mumming*, *A Pint of Murder*, and *The Grub-and-Stakers Move a Mountain*.